I0647909

A Divine Christmas Ghost Story

BOOK II

Copyright © 2022 Robert Cameron Malcolm IV

All rights reserved. No part of this book may be used or reproduced in any manner whatsoever without written permission of the author. Published 2022.

Printed in the United States of America.
ISBN: 978-1-63385-463-5
Library of Congress Control Number: 2022914672
Illustration by: Teresa Emeloff

Layout and Design by Jason Price

Published by:
Word Association Publishers
205 Fifth Avenue
Tarentum, Pennsylvania 15084

www.wordassociation.com
1.800.827.7903

A Divine Christmas Ghost Story

BOOK II

Robert Cameron Malcolm IV

Illustrations by: Teresa Emeloff

Acknowledgements

Once more a special thank you goes out to two very significant people in my life whose help with this book is truly most valuable and much appreciated: Jeffrey Andrew Yeager and Teresa Emeloff.

Jeff, my college roommate and lifelong friend, not only provided critical review of this story, but also performed the task of editing. His comments and suggestions, as always, were very helpful.

I am also indebted to Teresa Emeloff, a Highlands School District art teacher, for once again providing me with marvelous illustrations featured on the first page of each chapter. Her assistance with helping me get the word out about all the books I have written has been a Godsend.

I am also thankful for the help of The Reverend Jeffrey Scott Wylie, Rector of Christ's Church (ACNA) in Greensburg, Pennsylvania. His help and encouragement aided my effort in developing this story. I also deeply appreciate his help in publicizing all of the books I have written.

Thanksgiving goes out to my friend and former youth group assistant, Ray Kerr of Tarentum for his help in answering some questions of mine concerning this book.

While most of this tale is mythological, there is some historical truth behind parts of the story. The characters of John Robert MacCallum and Isabella Elizabeth McLagan represent my great, great grandparents, John and Isabella McLagan Malcolm who emigrated from the Perth/Dundee area of Scotland to the United States following the War Between the States. John Robert MacCallum, as a composite character, also represents his son, my great grandfather, Robert Cameron Malcolm. Portions of their story also represent some life experiences of my own. Stuart George Duckstein and Danielle Dayanna Gadberry represent my great uncle and aunt, George Donnell Stuart and Mary Edna Tench Stuart of Tarentum, Brackenridge, Leechburg, and Natrona Heights. Much of what is written about the development of their relationship in this novella is actual history. Dwayne Wright Chapman and his wife, Lucy, represent real life characters in the history of Tarentum of pharmacist and store owner, Dwight Chapman and his wife, Lucille. Dwight Chapman was a very kind and remarkable individual. The building that housed his pharmacy still stands at the southern corner of Fifth Avenue and Lock Street. Both "Chappie" and George Scheid were among the best friends of George D. Stuart at the former Valley Daily News and in the life of the Tarentum community.

It must be noted, that while *The Church of the Incarnation and the Saints of Advent* is purely mythological, Natrona Heights does have an Anglican Church of North America (ACNA) in the town. *Christ Our Hope Anglican Church* is located on Painter Avenue. Father John Bailey is its rector. None of the happenings written in this story reflect anything associated with that fine congregation.

Finally, I deeply appreciate Tom and Francine Costello, Jason Price, and April Urso of Word Association Publishers, Tarentum, PA, for all their encouragement, suggestions, and help. They are absolutely terrific to work with and do a marvelous job in assisting their authors.

Dedication

This book is dedicated to my marvelous wife, Laurie Ann Wright Malcolm. Laurie has taught me more about love than any other person with the exception of the Christ.

This book is also dedicated to my two adopted granddaughters, Jillian and Danielle, with whom I am well pleased!

Contents

Preface

his book represents a sequel to my 2021 novella entitled, *A Divine Christmas Ghost Story.* I had no intention of writing another story similar to that one. The truth of the matter is that a couple plot lines ran through my head after publishing the above story. I took one of these two plot lines and developed it into the tale you find in this book. The outline of the story came together rapidly. I also decided to highlight my home communities of Freeport, Natrona Heights, Brackenridge, and Tarentum within the tale. Some of my character development derives from some leading citizens of the area in years past, as well as two fine individuals today. This book was fun to write as I combined aspects of the greater Christmas season, Halloween, spiritual warfare, and my own creative thinking into another positive tale about clergy and their churches.

Besides the entertainment value of this story, a greater purpose of the book is to provoke some thought and commentary on church and culture during this time in American and world history. It is my hope that some of the biblical teaching, church tradition, and speculation about life after this life highlighted here will be helpful to the reader.

To quote Charles Dickens, "I have endeavoured, in this ghostly little book, to raise the Ghost of an Idea,....May it haunt their houses pleasantly and no one wish to lay it!"

Stave 1

ᴚhe ᴚrees Have Eyes

In all of God's amazing, mysterious, expansive and lovely Creation, many times it is the small exertions that are initiated on the human scene that are determinative. Such was the godly experience and heavenly entreaties of one – John Robert MacCallum.

John Robert MacCallum was a quiet man whose life was totally unextraordinary. He lived and worked so as to call no attention to himself. He enjoyed living in the backwaters of this life where his presence raised no praise or concern. Taking up the trade of a shoemaker at a young age in Perth, Scotland, his advancing skill and creative design produced for himself a certain notoriety among those of the city on the banks of the River Tay. Citizens of both low-birth and nobility came to appreciate his craftsmanship, the quality of his labor, his honest demeanor, and his winsome personality. His tiny shop became a place of destination for many seeking quality footwear and leather goods. This included Alexander McLagan, his fair wife, Jane, and their lovely daughter Isabella Elizabeth. The trio came to his shop, not infrequently, to shoe their feet adorned by his comfortable and stylish wares.

John possessed some height, sported a stylish mustache, and was certainly considered to be handsome by all accounts. He was strong and muscular and certainly caught the eye of many a fair lady. Young women of courting age would frequent his shop, even when they were not seriously considering making a purchase, just to feast their eyes on this man they considered to be chiseled by the gods. This included the young Isabella McLagan. Isabella was a woman of great fortitude and determination. She was charming, attractive, and conversant. She made it her business to visit John's establishment at every opportunity and to engage him in conversation. Being a woman of some intelligence, there was substance in their communication with each other. They also discovered, as their friendship grew, that they shared many of the same religious and spiritual values and tenets. It did not take long for their curiosity in, and their growing esteem for the other, to bud into a delightful mutual fancy. This shared reverie, which they both individually and privately entertained, soon sparked and ignited a dream world of possibilities uttered only in their own personal midnight confessions. They spoke their growing attraction and all-consuming love for the other to no one, including each other.

In spite of John's interest in keeping a low-profile in life, his work and person had engendered the esteem of the community and the admiration of many a young woman. Trouble, which he earnestly desired to avoid in his life, now came knocking not only on the door of his heart, but to the threshold of his very establishment. One day Isabella arrived early to his shop, and amid tears announced that her parents had arranged for her to marry a certain local nobleman. It was a union that would produce status, wealth, and security for her. It was a union which many a young girl in those times might prefer, but not Isabella. Isabella could not and would not consent to the family plan. The very thought of it made her sick to her stomach. Had she no voice and vote in this whole vile transaction, and in the dealings of her family with her very person and life? She considered this whole affair thrust upon her as a great personal affront and violation. Obedience to her parents and to her family were deeply embedded in her psyche and the traditions of Scottish culture, but her mind could not rationalize away what she felt in her heart for John. Though no words of affection had passed between them, she believed that he had a loving interest in her. She blamed his shyness and reserve for his lack, thus far, of a forthright declaration of his intentions toward her. She also believed that marriage was for love. She asserted that it was defined as such in the Bible, and particularly expressed this way in Solomon's Song. Love, she reasoned, is the greatest gift one person could grant to another, and she wanted to give her gift only to John if he were willing to receive it. To be, by force or custom, unable to share her favor with the object of her affection was something she could not, and would not, tolerate.

As Isabella explained the new circumstances that now targeted her, John removed his apron and drew nigh to her clasping both of her arms, just below her shoulders, within his hands. Looking down at her, he knew it was time to properly express his innermost feelings and thoughts toward her. He told her that he loved her with all his heart. He asked her that if she felt the same, would she agree to be wed, and due to the situation, as soon as possible. Isabella expressed her love right back at him and concurred with his sentiment to marry immediately. The two gripped each other in a tight embrace – a long embrace - and then shared a very passionate, but resolute first kiss.

That evening, John visited with his two brothers, James and Peter MacCallum, at James' house in Methven. He informed them of the situation that now swirled around Isabella and himself. He and his brothers put their heads together and attempted to come up with a solution and a plan that could be well executed. In this they succeeded. Knowing that Isabella's father, Alexander, would never consent to his daughter marrying so far beneath her, the plan was to steal her away, present themselves immediately before a clergyman, and take flight to start a new life in America. Peter, James, and John pulled together all the monetary resources they could muster in the following days. John and Isabella would need transit money to the States, as well as funds to re-establish themselves. Isabella agreed with the plan and prepared herself for a quick exit. The scheme was for John and his brothers, at a prescribed hour on a selected night, to show up with a ladder and extract Isabella from her second-floor bedroom window. While James secured the ladder and Peter stood guard with an unsheathed sword, John would ascend the rungs and help his love and her belongings descend to street level. On the fourth day of December, 1863, the plan became operative. James, Peter, and John quietly, secretly, and successfully extracted Isabella from her house after midnight. Later that morning, John and Isabella were united in marriage at the Clunie Church on the west bank of Loch Clunie. Saying farewell to James and Peter, John and Isabella caught a boat in Dundee, on the Firth of Tay, that would help them reach Portsmouth on the English Channel and a voyage, in spite of the War Between the States, to America.

Surviving the voyage across the Atlantic Ocean, the couple disembarked in Philadelphia making their way to Indiana, Pennsylvania, and eventually to Freeport at the confluence of the Allegheny River and Buffalo Creek. The couple were able to purchase some land above Freeport in Allegheny County. John tried his hand at farming, but also worked in Freeport for the railroad and the municipality. Isabella bore John a number of children. Their life together was not financially lucrative, but the couple loved each other greatly and managed their affairs well.

John had a small farm in which he raised and pastured some animals, grew some crops, cultivated a tiny vineyard, and planted two little orchards. It was more than enough to keep him quite occupied. While John rose early in the morning to start his work, he loved the sights and sounds of twilight and the earth settling down to sleep. Located on the eastern most part of his land was a promontory from which one could look down upon the sleepy town of Freeport and the southwestern flow of the Allegheny River which shimmered at night in the starlight. John came here in the evenings over his many years to share his thoughts with God, to petition heaven, to meditate, and to reflect. During the winter, John imagined that he was looking down on Bethlehem as he enjoyed the twinkling lights below him. He imagined the shepherds in the field and the heralds who pronounced Christ's birth. It was easy for him to translate his imagination into thoughts of a spiritual kind. Yet early on John discovered, often in some of the most surprising ways, that God would not be found wanting or absent from him in this place. Truly, as the Bible reveals, the God of Jesus is a "with me God." God, to John, was one's life traveler – a guide on one's road through this world whose goal was to get one to God's appointed "journey's end" for each of God's saints. Some of the most surprising thoughts he ever encountered dawned on him during his evening prayer time. It was as if God, his travelling companion, was also his intimate spiritual counselor. John envisioned himself as God's pupil in what he often referred to as "the school of God." What he learned, he also shared in his service and stewardship through both church and community. There was one night, in particular, wherein John believed that God bathed him in an unfathomable amount of divine love to reveal to him the height, breadth, and depth of this aspect of the celestial nature and persona.

There was also one night in which John believed that God exposed him to what the reality of this world would be like without God's love, presence, and shepherding care. John felt as if he was surrounded and captured by evil. He felt as if the trees had eyes hiding a malevolence that wished him and all of God's own great ill and harm. This mystical experience of God's personal removal and absence absolutely terrified him. When it occurred, he was standing in the open field section of the promontory. All about him he imagined evil watching his every move and trying to apprehend and manipulate his every thought. Around he turned again and again, looking for release and deliverance as malevolence seemed to press in upon him from every direction. His distress was only relieved when the Spirit reappeared and took authority over the environment. He knew instantly what God was doing and what God was teaching him. The lesson that God wanted John to learn about divine preservation and the perseverance of the saints had been achieved. "Is this what really lurks in this world without God's intervening and overarching watchman-ship," he thought to himself? "This must be the meaning of hell," he also concluded. Yet, this location was always his own personal paradise. It was to him a private garden wherein he walked and talked with his divine Savior and Lord. It was, to him, a "thin place." The concept of a "thin place" derives from the Celtic spiritual understanding of a location wherein an encounter with God seems to be more likely, and the divine Spirit much more communicative. It is the idea of a locality on Earth wherein God can be more readily discovered, entertained, and engaged. Yes, this was truly a "thin place" to John. John, however, understood that the faith passed down to him had both an individual and corporate component. As a result, he dreamed that this land of his might become available some day for more people to share in encounters with the divine Being as he, himself, had so thoroughly enjoyed, and which had enriched his life in his new home country. He privately and prayerfully dedicated this piece of his property, with a sharp understanding of Christian stewardship, to God and God's people. His request of God was that someday, if in accord with the Holy Will, that a church might be erected on this site so that others could share in the fruit of God's presence just as he had come to know it in this locale.

It must be noted, however, that whenever something good, wholesome, and altogether excellent appears, often an opposing spoiling effect is not long in its attendance as well. Peace and respite, it must be known, were not the only experiences John would encounter in this place. John would also come to the promontory during the day when pausing from his labor and seeking the shade of one of the hilltop's trees. On one occasion as he sat down and rested under a large hardwood tree during a particularly hot day, he suddenly sensed a presence suspended above him. As he cocked his head back and looked up to get a better view he discovered, much to his horror, a big black snake slithering down the tree toward him. Alarmed, he swiftly rolled to his side and was quick to his feet as the monster found a hole in the tree and disappeared rapidly within. This wasn't the only frightening encounter he had in his own little paradise. On another day, while walking under an aged crabapple tree to his favorite place to sit and view the valley before him, a heavy articulated weight suddenly fell upon his shoulders and head from above. Instantly, he realized, much to his horror, that another long and thick slithering monster had gone airborne and had descended upon him. Terrified, he threw the serpent off his trembling body and dashed some paces away. Looking back, he observed that the brute had come from a branch high in the tree wherein it had captured a blue jay in its deadly maw. In trying to devour the bird, the serpent had unintentionally fallen upon him. These experiences led John to the realization that in every garden a snake lurks to rob, steal, and destroy our joy. John came to affirm that paradise, no matter how splendid, could be invaded by evil. Evil, and the disturbance and disruption it causes in our lives, must be confronted, resisted, and cast out. John affirmed that this task, in this era of divine/human reality, is a work of necessity given to us by heaven. It is the responsibility of each and every one of God's saints to thwart and foil evil's sinister designs. It is God's intention that God's people would engage, combat, and vanquish evil's various manifestations, including incarnations, if such semblance so appeared.

This story and these observations must be known and entertained by the reader. They form the backdrop of our extraordinary little tale which takes place more than a century later on this very piece of land that John MacCallum affirmed to be holy ground, whose possession he reasoned, was in contention by both heaven and heaven's adversaries. The truth of the current human era is that whatever good benefit our divine Majesty attempts to produce, opposition to Providence by heaven's enemies is mounted to spoil, lay waste, and destroy. The battle lines are drawn. And so, begins our story of foreboding, resistance, and resilience. May God strengthen you and bless you as you proceed.

Stave 2

The Church of The Incarnation and the Saints of Advent

Jeffrey James Fairlamb was born and grew up in Western Pennsylvania. His father was a steel worker in the Monongahela Valley for the U.S. Steel Corporation. His mother, besides being a homemaker, also worked in banking for the Pittsburgh National Corporation, which is known locally as PNC Bank. Jeffrey grew up devoted to God and the Roman Catholic expression of the Christian faith. He was so dedicated to God and God's Christ, that he believed that the divine Spirit was calling him to devote his life to the service of the Church. Jeffrey entered seminary and graduated with high honors. There was just one thing that stood in his way of serving the Church in the capacity of a Roman Catholic priest. Jeff was most tentative in terms of taking and fulfilling the vow of celibacy. It was not that he disagreed with this lifestyle, or had any extraordinary difficulty dealing with lust and sexual urges. It was none of these things at all, for Jeff was a very moral, ethical, and upstanding individual who was not easily led by temptation into the moral uncertainties of this time in human culture and history. Rather, our young seminarian who had a heart full of love for God, God's established order and dictates, and God's people, also possessed an inclination and desire to share his heart and innermost life with a young lady who also embodied his principles and beliefs. Jeff wanted a wife and a family. He could not deny this yearning of his mind and heart, and so, after graduation he did not pursue ordination into the priesthood. He took up secular employment and with his sharp mind and personal skills performed his tasks with great proficiency.

Jeff was a very handsome man with an attractive personality. He was not a tall individual, but possessed fine features. He was witty, enjoyed quality humor, and was absolutely delightful. He could be a bit adventurous. He enjoyed pursuits that stretched his personhood and abilities, and which added to the library of his knowledge and his experiential resume. In the way the world qualifies things, Jeff had a lot going for him. There were just two things that eluded him: a quality relationship with a fair lady; and an inner burning desire to serve God and God's people in a more profound manner.

In his search for greater spiritual identity and fulfillment, Jeff began attending, and later united with, a Presbyterian Church. He formed a solid bond with the clergyman who served the Church, and found enrichment in the biblical presentation there and in many aspects of Reformed theology. This, however, only intensified his desire to serve the Lord in a clerical way. Balancing both Catholic and Reformed perspectives on his faith, he explored and then sought admission into the newly formed Anglican Church of North America. He was enthusiastically accepted as a candidate for this expression of the Anglo-Catholic priesthood, and completed the additional seminary studies he needed in order to qualify for ordination as an ACNA clergyperson.

During and after his completion of seminary, he served under the tutelage of the rector of Christ's Church in Greensburg, Pennsylvania. He participated in several other ministry opportunities as well. Father Fairlamb grew in both his abilities and in wisdom. He was recognized as an up-and-coming young priest. His superiors came to believe that he could handle a real challenge in ministry. Little did Jeff know that a significant opportunity to display his skills was rapidly coming his way.

Father Fairlamb never heard of John Robert MacCallum. He knew nothing about him, his land which the following generations of his family still possessed, or his prayer which would set the course for the rest of Jeff's ministry and life. An interfacing of time, people, and the divine Will was about to commence.

During this period of time in church history in America, a significant amount of change and disruption was taking place. There was a split in the Episcopal Church which led to the birth of the conservative Anglican Church in North America. Presbyterians, Lutherans, Methodists, and many other bodies of the historically time-honored denominations in the United States were also going through difficult disruptions and disagreements. Many people were left disillusioned and disgruntled. Some people simply dropped out of church membership and involvement. Others found alternative church expressions in which to worship, but kept their participation limited. Still others, undaunted by the new religious and cultural circumstances, wished to form alliances and birth church institutions more conducive to their viewpoints and spiritual expectations. It was in this milieu that the "Church of the Incarnation and the Saints of Advent" was birthed with an affiliation to the ACNA denomination. So many churches in the Allegheny-Kiskiminetas River Valleys sported in their corporate legal identity the names "Harvest", "River", and "Community". Those who founded the "Church of the Incarnation and the Saints of Advent" wanted to lift up both a significant theological identity as well as to honor some of the best brothers and sisters in church history. The name was surely a bit cumbersome, but the originators believed that this church must broadcast a clarion call to people who live between the first coming and the anticipated second coming of the Savior and Lord Jesus Christ.

Due to a trio of wealthy donors turned off by the changes in their former denominational allegiances, the decision was made to cast their lot with the ACNA and plant a new church development in the northernmost part of Natrona Heights. The group was impressed with the Anglican church's dedication to both the Word and Christ. They were also impressed with the ACNA's dedication to tradition and the ethics derived from Scripture. The trio, and those who joined them, developed seven standards they wanted to secure in the establishment of a new church development. These seven were: the emphasis on the "R" word – "Relationship" – meaning that the divine/human connection was one in which both parties desired an intimate and eternal love affinity one with the other; a church centered upon an educated emphasis of the 66 books of the Bible; a church which emphasized solid theological standards; a church that was steeped in a quality biblical and theological educational orientation; a church that was mission oriented; a church that could bridge the gap between a high church expression and the evangelical; and a church that would guide and challenge current cultural standards and not surrender to them. The trio, and those who joined them, did not want to erect a steel box building. They did not want to worship in an edifice that would also function as a gymnasium. They wanted a church founded on solid architectural standards. They desired a church that elevated the spirit in terms of aesthetics. They wished for a church with a lofty roof and a spire or tower which pointed to the heavens. They longed for a church with comfortable pews rather than movable chairs. In short, they wanted a church that looked like a church, felt like a church, and inspired lofty thoughts like those built down through the centuries in both Europe and America. The construction of such a building in these days was very expensive. The stone edifice that was designed and crafted would not house a large sanctuary. It was more like a quaint chapel that featured a tall tower with a flat roof – one from which a person could view the splendor of the valley and river below. The tower became an enhancement on the grand view that John MacCallum so enjoyed. Instead of stately stained-glass windows, clear panes offered a view to the towering trees and the woods surrounding the church on three sides. As it turned out, the church made an impressive presentation on top of the hill amid the tiny forest.

Interestingly enough, one of the founders was a descendant of John Robert MacCallum. He donated a portion of his land, formerly John Robert's property, for the fulfillment of this project. He knew nothing of MacCallum's aspiration, prayer, and dedication, and yet he gave the very piece of land John Robert had envisioned for a future congregation. It is often said that the "Lord works in mysterious ways". It might be better to say that God honors the aspirations of the saints of old and is not limited by the hands of time.

After much planning, the church came into fruition with a driveway to the promontory which included an upper and lower parking lot. The lengthy name that was chosen for the new church focused both on the beginning of God's one work in Jesus Christ which wrought humanity salvation, and the subsequent human response to God's amazing gift. It was no accident that the church's founders wanted a church based on the Nativity with an emphasis on the seasons of Advent, Christmas, and Epiphany, while looking forward to the glory of Easter. In fact, the mission statement of the Church which the founders crafted read much like the translated American lyrics, by the Rev. John Sullivan Dwight in 1855, to the Christmas carol, "O Holy Night." It was to this new church development that Fairlamb was called to be the first rector. Little did he know the blessings and the challenges that awaited him as he began his first day of service as vicar. Right from the start, it was going to be quite a ride!

Stave 3

The Beautiful Language and a Lover's Concerto

On the first day of his employment, at 9 in the morning, Jeffrey James Fairlamb was greeted by a small crowd of well-wishers and church employees as he entered the building and began to proceed to his office. All of them were looking forward to getting to know him better and to serve alongside of this recently elected pastor. Among them was Jillian Julianna Jiganie. Jillian served as the organist/choir director for the new church development. Jillian was charming, effervescent, bright, and radiated optimism and a can-do spirit. She caught Jeffrey's eye immediately, as she was slender, possessed long flowing brown hair, and was altogether lovely. In fact, she was the very definition of the appellation, "the Queen of Cuteness". Her smile not only lit up a room, but it was very disarming as well. She possessed a pleasing personality and was a most cooperative individual. Her temperament and disposition sometimes got her into trouble with others as she could be quick to criticize. She was, however, no one's fool and was swift to defend herself and justify her actions. She was talented on the organ and the piano, and was proficient with a number of other instruments, among them the flute and the piccolo. Hired right out of Penn State University, she had great aspirations for her career in education. She had also studied psychology and thought that picking up a school counselor position might be the right fit for her. She also was excited about her part-time job at *The Church of the Incarnation and the Saints of Advent.*

Jillian descended from families sharing Austrian, Hungarian, and Romanian descent. She grew up as a person of faith and expressed a deep regard for her Lord and Savior, Jesus Christ. She was single and unattached. It was amazing that while in college, a young man had not discovered her and snatched her up and away. She was, however, looking for a lasting relationship with a man who shared her faith. She wanted someone who would be loyal, trustworthy, and true. She was a genuine romantic who desired to be creatively loved and appreciated. It must be stated here that both Jeffrey and Jillian took note of each other on Jeff's first day.

One could not say that the initial sparks of attraction fired off on this their introduction, but there was also nothing that took place which discouraged a future consideration of affection. The two were charged to work together to help build up church attendance through the conduct of quality worship services, special service offerings, concerts, and other musical expressions. Their initial meeting and discussion that day was an encouraging and a fruitful one for them both. One thing was most certain, they developed an instantaneous liking for each other.

Now Jeff was a popular individual who developed friendships easily. To The Church of the Incarnation, he brought with him a couple of his friends who lived in the Allegheny-Kiski Valley. One of his best friends was Stuart George Duckstein. George was a gregarious individual who was very sharp and blessed with a definite intellectual advantage vis-à-vis most people. George was not an overly handsome man, but he was very attentive, patient, cool under fire, and always present when needed. On top of all these attributes, he was incredibly romantic, and honestly so, but thus far in his young life this skill had not yet been established, witnessed, and noted. George also enjoyed self-deprecating humor and often referred to his physique as "my corpulent self." He was not only the epitome of Christian servanthood, but he was a man who never indulged in vice. He did not gamble. He did not partake of illicit drugs or overuse pharmaceuticals. He used no tobacco products, did not consume alcohol, and was never caught employing bad language. He did not swear and never, ever, took the Lord's name in vain. He was just about as upstanding a man as one could find in the Allegheny Valley. About the worst thing that he ever said, was his own self-designation as GD – or "George Damn". He often referred to himself this way and employed it in signing personal letters and, in some cases, the copy of freelance articles he wrote. GD was a writer and an editor, and a darn good one with a great sense of what was important and appropriate to record and what was not. He was also incredibly proficient with the King's English and a grammatical expert. At this time in his life, he was not interested in women and was a confirmed bachelor. He engaged in conversation with anyone who would listen to his opinion about the virtues and liberties that singleness afforded and in which he championed. He was never going to get hitched. No one, he believed, would ever strike his fancy. He determined to himself that he would always view these matters with the fairer sex in such a manner. Little did George know that he was about to meet his match in a most disarming way.

Another friend that Jeff cajoled into attending the Church of the Incarnation was Dwayne Wright Chapman. Dwayne, who was known to his best friends as "Chappie", was an affable and lovable fellow who was exceedingly kind to both children and dogs. He was employed as a pharmacist in Tarentum after attending the University of Pittsburgh. Chappie was a tall fellow with handsome features. Jeffrey and George both served in the wedding party when he married a woman named, Lucy. Dwayne always sported a big smile and became a very popular individual in Tarentum. Everyone trusted him and expressed the utmost confidence in him. Dwayne and Lucy were tremendous advocates of the Christian faith, and like George, brought great talent and resources to the Church of the Incarnation.

There is one additional individual whose value to this story is not insignificant. Her name is Danielle Dayanna

Gadberry. Danielle was a playmate and high school friend of Jillian Jiganie. Their mutual self-designation was "BFF" – "best friends forever". Danielle was very sharp intellectually. She was, in many respects, an All-American girl who was a great debater and excelled in the qualities of listening, analysis, and synthesis. She also was very talented in both music and dance. Though her ancestry was English, Irish, and Scottish, in high school and college she studied French, Spanish, Latin, and German. She was fluent in the first two of these. She shied away from a greater proficiency in the German language because she considered it to be too guttural. She possessed a deep affection for the rhyme, meter, and flow of the "romance languages". It must also be noted that Danielle enjoyed all things Celtic, and her favorite saint was Nicholas. Danielle graduated in the top five of her high school class and was Summa Cum Laude in college. As a new high school teacher, she taught both French and English. Danielle was very sweet, but she could also be a bit standoffish and short spoken with people. She did not tolerate stupidity and foolishness on the part of others very well. This caused some people to think that she was a bit stuck-up and full of herself.

Danielle could be a very charming and captivating individual in the right circumstances. Like Jillian, Danielle was not tall. Also, like Jillian, Danielle was very pretty and had beautiful blue eyes. Unlike Jillian, Danielle instead had long flowing blonde hair. Men found her looks to be quite alluring, but her intellectual acumen caused many a man to shy away from her. Children, however, just adored her and were much attracted to her person. As a Christian, Jillian believed that Danielle would fit in well at the Church of the Incarnation in children's ministry, and was attempting to recruit her to form an elementary youth group called "The Jesus Bunch". At this point in our story, however, Danielle had not yet assented to participation in ministry at "CTI", as the "Church of the Incarnation" was often referred to by some. This all was about to change, and quickly so. Yes, as it would turn out, she would find a home at the *Church of the Incarnation and the Saints of Advent*.

Father Jeff began his pastorate in the late spring of the calendar year. During the summer season, besides getting acquainted with the people of his parish, he began to chart and flesh out the coming ministry year. The new ministry or program year would begin on the Sunday following Labor Day. This was the custom in many churches. Father Fairlamb wanted to get as much of a jump on the season as he could, so he called a number of meetings with his staff which took place throughout the summer. Since the number of staff members and volunteers was small, due to the fact that the church was new and its membership tiny, he began to count heavily on Jillian. At one early summer meeting between the two of them he said, "Jillian, this church was given its name in celebration of the Incarnation of Jesus Christ in the womb of Mary. The name also recognizes the saints of the church as celebrated during the Advent season. We need to take this opportunity to emphasize and highlight both the saints and the Nativity. We need to do this more than any other church in our region during the upcoming greater holiday season. Every church needs to have a niche in the community. Every church needs to find one, or two, or three things at most, that can be done well and for which they can become renowned in their area. The way we celebrate the seasons, particularly Advent, Christmas, and Epiphany is one thing we can certainly emphasize. This could make a positive impression on the community. Through it, we could become, as I have already stated, well known in this valley."

"I agree with you, Father Jeff. We can celebrate a saint-filled Christmas which can help illuminate the coming of the Christ," replied Jillian.

"Whatever we do, Jillian, we must celebrate Christmas well!" emphasized Jeff.

"Do you know what really bothers me about the way most people celebrate the Christmas season?", asked Jillian.

"No, what?" asked Jeff.

"I think that people, and certainly our culture, has a tendency to over-emphasize Advent, to the detriment of Christmastide," asserted Jillian. "Think about it for a minute - most people, and many families, host Christmas events up through Christmas Day, and that's it! How many people get to the close of the day on the 25th and then sink into a depression because the holiday is now over. I know people who take down their tree and all their decorations on the 26th. Have you ever noticed that on December 26 all the Christmas music vanishes from the radio? Christmas was meant to be celebrated for 12 days. It is during the 12 days that the feasting, gatherings, and parties are to be held. It is during the 12 days when well-wishing and visiting should take place. We have got the proverbial cart before the horse. Today, we celebrate Advent as if it were Christmas. Advent is supposed to be a season of reflection and preparation for the coming of the Christ. A colleague of mine in Ohio wrote to me last year about this very observation. He stated this in his e-mail, 'The secular world packages up Christmas and puts it in storage until next October. The Church should be celebrating Christmas for 12 days. The Word made flesh and dwelt among us is far too important to stuff in a box because the so-called culturally designated Holiday Season is over.' Don't you agree with him?"

"I certainly do," replied Fairlamb. "In fact, in Bavaria and other parts of Germany, the Holiday or Christmas Season begins on Saint Andrew's Day which is November 30th. It only ends on the Octave of Epiphany, which is January 13. That's 45 days in which to celebrate the season. Some traditions even celebrate it through Candlemas on February 2nd. Candlemas, of course, is the remembrance of the presentation of Jesus at the Temple by Joseph and Mary as based on Luke 2:22-40."

"I am, being part Austrian, aware of Bavarian and German traditions. I like them. I agree with them. If this is the direction you would like to go, I am 100% with you on this," exclaimed Jillian.

"So, you are Austrian," replied Fairlamb.

"Yes, my ancestors came from Austria, but also Hungary and Romania. In fact, my last name is Romanian," stated Jillian.

"Interesting," replied Fairlamb.

"Yeah," Jillian continued, "I sometimes get teased because of my name. Since all three of my names start with 'J' people have given me all sorts of nicknames."

"Like what?" instantly inquired Jeffrey.

"Oh, like 'Jaybird', 'Triple J', 'JJ', and even 'Triple J Ranch' as if I was somehow 'Wrangler Jane' from the Old West," stated Jillian with a disturbing frown on her face.

"Interesting," replied Fairlamb once more. "How would you prefer me to address you?"

"You can refer to me by my proper name or even 'Jilly' if you desire," replied Jiganie.

"Either 'Jillian' or 'Jilly' would be fine with me," declared Fairlamb with a broad smile on his face.

Their eyes caught each other. Fairlamb noticed what beautiful blue eyes Jillian had and for a moment drank deeply of them. Perhaps the first notion of possibility in terms of a romantic connection on their parts flashed between them in this time seemingly suspended in space. Realizing that he was staring at her, Jeffrey quickly broke away and said, "Let's continue thinking about the coming seasons including the autumnal season as well, shall we? What else can we come up with?"

"Well," said Jillian, "We need to sponsor services and events that will attract people and meet their needs. I think we should emphasize 'All Saints' Day' as well as conduct a Thanksgiving Eve service. Hardly anyone in this valley sponsors a Thanksgiving Eve service. Such a service might be fun to do and we could get very creative with it. What do you think?"

"I like where your mind is going," replied Fairlamb. "Between All Saints and Thanksgiving, we could also emphasize Veterans' Day with a special remembrance service of the end of the war to 'end all wars' as it was once upon a long time ago referred to."

"We could share that on the Sunday before Veterans' Day," stated Jillian. "Concerning Advent and the saints, if November 30th is the start of the Christmas season in Germany, that should be our jumping off point as well – of course – whichever comes first – St. Andrew's Day or the First Sunday of Advent."

"Yes, we could call it St. Andrew's Sunday," declared Father Jeff, "and employ banners and flags and highlight the person and mission of St. Andrew."

"Wasn't Andrew the disciple in the Gospels who was always bringing people to Jesus?" asked Jillian.

"That's right," exclaimed Fairlamb, "we could call all those who introduce people to Jesus as being members of the 'Andrew Society'."

"Anglicans celebrate St. Thomas on the day of the winter solstice, do they not?" inquired Jillian.

"Yes, Saint Thomas' Day for us is December 21, normally the day of the solstice," replied Fairlamb. "Let me see, we could celebrate Saint Barbara's Day."

"Saint Barbara, who is she?" asked Jillian.

"She is the saint of lightning and fireworks, a martyr from what today is the country of Turkey," replied Father Jeff. "Her story is a very interesting one, but also a very sad one as well."

"That could open us up to some interesting possibilities," exclaimed Jillian in an excited manner.

"Two days after Saint Barbara's Day which is December 4th, is Saint Nicholas' Day, the original gift giver. We could also include Saint Ambrose's Day on December 7th and Saint Lucy's Day on the 13th. Saint Lucia of Syracuse was a martyr in the Diocletianic Persecution. I know that other traditions celebrate some other saints during December as well. Some of them may not be appropriate for us, but we can look into it," said Father Jeff.

"I know that the Feast of St. Stephen is normally held on the 26th of December," quickly added Jillian. "That day is not in Advent, but we could do something to remember and celebrate it as well in that it is part of the Christmas season. And please remember that Saint John the Apostle and Evangelist, the son of Zebedee and Salome, is celebrated the next day, December 27th."

"You are so right. Saint Stephen's Day is also 'Boxing Day' which has a long history in our tradition in the United Kingdom and in Canada. Boxing Day would be a wonderful time to highlight mission," exclaimed Jeff. "Saint John's Day is often missed in most church traditions. Very few people also know that the 28th is 'Holy Innocents Day' which recounts the slaughter by Herod's troops of the children in and around Bethlehem. We might be able to highlight that occasion as a day of remembrance in some somber and respectful way as well."

"We could also celebrate 'Twelfth Night', Father Jeff, on the last evening of Christmastide with a traditional style party like they had in yesteryear if we could just get people to come out for an evening of fun, food, and games," proffered Jillian. "We could substitute a New Year's Eve party for this ancient traditional event. Some kind of church dinner in the undercroft might work. As you know, serving food generally brings people out!"

"We have also got to think of what we could possibly do to end the whole season on the 'Octave', January 13," Fairlamb added.

Breaking their train of thought, Jeff stated thoughtfully, "This has been a great meeting. We have much more thinking to do, but I like where we are headed. One more thing, Jillian, you do not have to address me as 'Father Jeff' or 'Father Fairlamb' every time you talk to me. Please, just call me 'Jeff'."

"I was wondering, if you don't mind me asking you," queried Jillian, "if anyone has ever made fun of your last name."

"Yes, they have," responded Jeff, "but I love my last name. It reminds me of Jesus, 'the lamb of God that takes away the sins of the world.' It also reminds me of one of my favorite hymns, 'Fairest Lord Jesus'. My family name is one that I love in spite of what the crass and crude of our culture might suggest. Speaking of nicknames, people have referred to me as 'JJ' and even 'Jesse James', but please, you can call me 'Jeff.' I do not think we need to be formal with each other. I am not going to refer to you as 'Organist Jiganie' or "Choir Director Jillian' – so please just use my first name, and as people around here used to say, 'that's it, Fort Pitt!'"

"Certainly, and thank you," replied Jillian giggling a little.

With smiles on their faces, Jillian left Jeff's office. They were both developing a great deal of respect for each other, but more than that, a significant connection between them was coming to flower as well.

Things went well for Father Jeff and for CTI through the summer and early in the autumnal season. Slowly, but surely, the worship attendance on Sunday morning was growing. A Middle School youth group and a High School youth group were initiated. While, the number of attending youth was small, both groups were off to a good start with Father Jeff in charge. In Christian Education, a church school was started, a couple small study and prayer groups were instituted, and plans were in the works for an elementary youth group and a summer Vacation Bible School. Jillian was able to re-cruit a small choir and employed her instrumental skills in the church's worship services. Her boldness in seeking out and communicating with musicians in the Pittsburgh area helped her to line up performers for the coming holiday sea-son. She also desired to eventually start a handbell choir and a children's choir, and was working toward this end. Father Jeff talked her into assisting him with the youth groups. As it turned out, she became his most capable and reliable assistant. This caused the two of them to spend a great deal of time with each other which furthered the development of their friendship. Jillian was still trying to convince her best friend, Danielle, to attend and get involved in the church. Thus far, Jillian's efforts had not borne fruit. It was, however, another unanticipated connection that brought Danielle into the fold. Once again one could say, that God works in mysterious ways. Maybe it would be better to say that God is not frustrated by our repeated hesitancy to serve, but maneuvers circumstances to secure the divine desire. If such is the case in God's realm, one must think about affirming the divine validity of what appears to be the frequency of coincidences which lead to blessing.

Danielle became involved in CTI due to her response to an article that Stuart George Duckstein wrote that was printed in the local newspaper. George wrote an article critical of some aspects of public education policy. Danielle responded by writing a letter to the editor countering a couple of his assertions. Her erudition was so sharp and exacting that George was stunned that someone could best him in his arguments and assertions. George became more than curious about this woman and asked his fellow editor, a man commonly referred to as Scheidy, if he knew who she was. He responded that she was an instructor for the Highlands School District and that he had recently been introduced to her. "Do you want me to arrange a meeting?" Scheidy asked him. "Sure, I would like to see if she is as intelligent as she appears to be," George responded curiously. So Scheidy set up an encounter with those whom he knew were Danielle's co-workers. They would arrange a dinner at the Tarentum Train Station restaurant, wherein Scheidy would arrive with

George. Danielle knew nothing of the set-up. Of course, George helped to formulate the plan.

Scheidy and George appeared at JG's Tarentum Station Grille on Sixth Avenue in the town at the intersection of the Allegheny River and Bull Creek at the appointed time. The two of them located the girls in the busy and conversation filled eatery walking over to their table for introductions. Was it love at first sight? We may never know, but the confirmed bachelor was instantly taken with her. He always explained the development of their relationship, at least at first, as one of an intellectual interest only. In reality, it was far more than that. In just one meeting, her personality, beauty, charm, and, of course her intellect, captured his manly heart. Immediately, he began scheming as to how he might spend time with her without being too obvious, particularly to her. As the reader has already been informed, George was not remarkable in his looks. He was – well, let's just say, pleasantly plump. And his curly hair was already beginning to recede. George Damn was, however, very clever. He had always wanted to learn French, which he called "the beautiful language". So, knowing where Danielle taught, he sought an audience with her during the after-school hours. Being escorted to her classroom, the school receptionist called out to Danielle saying, "You've got a visitor."

"Hello, Miss Gadberry, so this is your hallowed hall of erudition," remarked George trying bravely to put on his best face.

"Yes, this is my classroom. I am surprised to see you Mr. Duckstein, to what do I owe to your surprise visit into my sacred sanctuary?" queried Danielle.

"Well, I have always been interested in learning French. I was wondering if you could help me by letting me borrow a book so that I might begin my self-motivated study," responded George.

"Most certainly, good sir, I can loan you a book on beginner's French for you to study at home on your own," quickly stated Danielle.

"That would be wonderful, but please drop the more formal salutation of Mr. Duckstein, would you please?" requested George.

"Duckstein is an interesting last name, wouldn't you say so?" questioned Danielle. Before George could answer, Danielle retorted, "Your name reminds me of Mary Shelley's 'Frankenstein'. Has anyone ever called you 'Quackerstein' in jest? Yes, you could fashion a very unique Halloween costume for yourself. Don't you think? Please, understand I am not trying to insult you or go overboard in teasing you. Also, I do not consider you to be a 'quack.' I know that you are a very intelligent man and a quality reporter and writer. I do find, however, your last name to be quite unique!"

George offered no verbal reply. He just shrugged his shoulders not sure how to respond.

"How then do you want me to address you?" asked Danielle. "You have to admit that you have a very interesting name, I even hear that you go by 'George Damn' as well."

"Why yes, since my initials are 'GD', I think you can figure out where the appellation 'George Damn' comes from. I really just use it in jest," cried George. "I am not trying to be sacrilegious and blasphemous or anything like that, of course."

"Of course, well, that's also interesting because I have learned that your initials are SGD. What does the 'S' represent?" inquired Danielle.

"Oh, so you have been inquiring about me – interesting! To answer your question, I go by my middle name George, but my first name is Stuart," replied Mr. Duckstein.

"I thought so, because one member of the staff here told me your name is really and truly 'Stuart'," declared Danielle. "If you don't mind, I think I will refer to you as 'Stuey', or maybe just 'Tuey'. Do you mind? May I call you that?"

"I can be your 'Stuey' or 'Tuey' if you will do me one additional favor, for reimbursement of course. Will you tutor me in 'the beautiful language'? I think I would learn much faster if we could get together once a week for an hour or two of instruction," George said courageously and anxiously.

"Well, this is an interesting turn of events," exclaimed Danielle. "Yes, I guess so. I guess I can tutor you, but forget the remuneration. We can meet at the local coffee house or a restaurant and I would be pleased to grant you my expert instruction. You can pay for the coffee and dessert, if you please!"

Well, that was certainly fine with George. This had turned out better than he anticipated. As he left the school, he was ecstatic. He knew he had as good a chance as anyone to win her heart – all he needed was time to allow his personality and many qualities to charm her lovely spirit. And that is exactly what happened. And it happened in an amazingly short time period as well.

Since George was attending, and had become a member of CTI, in time he invited Danielle to worship with him. She answered in the affirmative and that is how she became involved in this Anglican church.

At the same time that a potent regard was budding and flowering between Danielle and George, a love explosion was also about to encompass Jillian and Jeffrey.

One night, as October eves were soon to surrender to November's chilly eventide, Jillian was practicing on the piano in the sanctuary when Jeff entered the nave. Jillian asked him, "Do you know how to read music, Jeff?'

"Yes, I can read music and I did take some piano lessons, but I was never very good. My piano teacher commented that I played with great feeling and expression, but I was never able to master sight reading. That was my downfall," responded the good Father.

"Well, come right here and sit down on this bench beside me," requested Jillian. "Have you ever played 'Heart and Soul' with anyone – ever?"

"No, I haven't," replied Jeffrey.

"Come on, let's play it together. I'll show you your notes. You can have the easy part," exclaimed Jillian.

"Ok, if you insist," stated Jeffrey.

Jeffrey sat down beside her. She gently placed her hand on his hand. The touch of her hand, ever so gentle on his, sent electricity pulsating through his entire body. Her touch was unlike any other he had ever experienced in his whole life. He couldn't concentrate on what she was attempting to show him. The notes were so confusing. All he could think about was the magical feel of her fingers on his. As she began to play, he fumbled badly his part. Quickly, he ceased his attempt to press the keys and enfolded his left hand around her right hand. He held it tightly, but dearly. Jillian stopped playing immediately. She exercised no restraint in attempting to remove her hand from his. He looked up from the keyboard and only inches away from her face, he stared deeply into those beautiful blue eyes of hers. She replicated the same motion. His vision now concentrated on her lips, so sweet and inviting and intensely irresistible he found them to be.

There was nothing in her expression that signaled a red stop light or any hesitancy or reluctance at all. While still resting on the ivory, their hands tightened their grasp on each other. Their heads then began a forward motion – inexorably moving closer and closer – until their lips touched. An instant surge of another shot of electricity coursed rapidly through Jeff's body. An electrical charge also raced through Jillian as well as the two of them fully embraced each other. They clung enveloped in the other as if someone had unexpectantly returned from the grave, so firm was their embrace. Their kiss was deep, passionate, and penetrating. Volumes of emotion pent up for weeks and months suddenly gushed out from their souls and found a vacant reservoir with which to fill, one in the other. Upon the inevitable separation of their lips, the two continued to cling to each other as if some magical glue had melded them together. Finally, separating after what seemed to be a protracted period of whimsy and fantasy, Jeffrey said to her, "Well, I guess we have some things to talk about, don't we?"

"Yes, I think we do," Jillian replied while bowing her head and smiling bashfully.

"I will be certain to call you later this evening if you don't mind," stated Jeff rather sheepishly. "I wish I didn't have this office call coming up in a matter of minutes, but I must retreat to my study."

"I understand," replied Jillian. "I will look forward to talking with you later."

Jeff slid slowly off the piano bench and made his way to his office. As he took each step, he realized more and more that he was in love. He was completely bewitched and enthralled by her. That certainly was his thought and conclusion in the afterglow of their passionate encounter. He was also, most of all, happy to have discovered and experienced such a state of ecstasy. What he did not know at that moment was that temptation was about to come his way. It was not, however, the kind of temptation he might have imagined it would be in his current state of exhilaration.

Stave 4
Temptation Eyes

It is a most sincere and sobering fact in today's world, that any success that goodness, virtue, and righteousness achieve attracts the attention of evil, the onslaught of opposition, and a counter response. Such is the case in the story of *The Church of the Incarnation and the Saints of Advent*. Father Jeffrey James Fairlamb and his newly formed congregation, though small, was gaining in godly might each and every week through the summer and autumnal seasons.

Unlike many churches whose influence does not represent any kind of a lethal threat to the wicked designs of the opponents of our good God, CTI's growing influence was attracting the wrong kind of attention. Evil was beginning to gather its resources to strike back and attempt to spoil any positive gains that heaven might secure in this place and among its people. As is so often the case, the plan was to pursue one or more of the so-called "Seven Deadly Sins."

The *Seven Deadly Sins* of church tradition and lore include greed, envy, anger, pride, sloth, gluttony, and lust. The forces of evil knew that male clergy are often susceptible to greed, pride, and lust. Often evil threw in gluttony as well, but this latter sin was more in the imagination of the media and ministerial detractors than evidenced in reality. The one sin that Evil thought Jeffrey James might be susceptible to was lust. After all, as a Roman Catholic he did not, and could not in all good conscience, take the vow of celibacy in order to enter the priesthood, and following his passionate escapade with Jillian on the piano bench, Satan's forces thought they might be able to entrap him in this way. And so, Evil devised a plan and enacted a strategy through a sharp, striking, and voluptuous woman named Ernaline Bedelia Kherington.

Ernaline's assault upon the base proclivity of the human instincts and passions of Jeffrey James commenced on Saint Andrew's Sunday as the congregation celebrated the First Sunday in Advent. Ernaline entered the sanctuary following the processional while Father Jeff was up front in the chancel area and could take note of her dramatic entry. Dressed in black in a well-fitted dress which featured her exceedingly curvaceous form, she strolled seductively down the aisle preparing to sit on the Gospel Ambo side of the sanctuary right in the first row of pews. CTI practiced, as many churches did even during an endemic, a ritual of friendship where a greeting, handshake, and hug could be exchanged. Father Jeff left the altar area and walked down the steps of the elevated chancel and was met quickly by Ernaline, who pressed herself against him in a rather forward embrace. In so doing he could feel her body squeezed up against his own. Such an action certainly gained his attention. It was one in which his mind took note as he, at the same time, attempted to break away. Some in the congregation noted this action, specifically Chappie, Lucy, George, Danielle, and most particularly, Jillian. Ernaline, on her part, was determined not to let him get away so fast. She grabbed his right hand with her left hand and his left arm with her right and proceeded to introduce herself. "My name is Ernaline, but you can call me 'Ernie'," she stated rather confidently. "I am very interested in learning more about your church, so maybe we can talk for a minute or two following the service." Jeff could not help but notice her sweet melodious voice and her long black hair which seemed to reach out toward him at every movement of her head. He also noticed her most pleasant perfumed scent. It was rather intoxicating. As he ascended back into the chancel, he remembered a quote from an old television comedy which offered the idea that "love enters through the nose." As he proceeded with the service, her scent lingered in his olfactory. His concentration was challenged as she sat before him crossed legged exposing a great deal of skin. Jillian, by no means blind and unknowing as to what was going on before her, was very displeased. Jeff managed to get through the service with only a limited number of errors due to the distraction right in front of him, but Jillian and those who knew him best realized that he was serving while a bit disturbed.

As Jeff left the chancel during the recessional, Ernaline smiled at him and followed him with her eyes. Jeff, very cognizant that he was being watched by many, made only a brief glance at her smiling respectfully, and then turned his attention to others as he recessed. Ernaline lingered in the sanctuary and only advanced to greet him when most of the worshippers had left. She said to him, "I really enjoyed your service, the music, and your words. You have a lovely church building here and an amazing congregation. I am certainly interested in learning more about your church. Could we get together very soon? The sooner the better. Do you, like many ministers, take Mondays off? If not, I could come by tomorrow to see you. If that is not satisfactory, how about we arrange a time for Tuesday? My schedule is pretty free. I can make myself available on any day and at any time you so desire."

"Well," stammered Jeff, "I have learned that I need to start my week's work early on Mondays in case anything unexpected comes along and bogs me down during the rest of the week. I can meet with you either tomorrow or on Tuesday."

"Tomorrow it is," Ernaline quickly interjected. "Would 10 AM be a good time for you to meet with me? I will come here to your office."

"Yes, that will be satisfactory," replied Jeff, realizing that Jillian had now approached the two of them and was intently listening to the conversation.

"10 O'clock then it is," asserted Ernaline with both delight and an air of confidence about her. "I will look forward to seeing you then! Have a dreamy day!"

At this, Ernaline proceeded to depart.

As Jillian and Jeffrey watched her go, Jillian turned and said to Jeff sternly, "You better watch yourself – you just better watch yourself with that one!" With that said, Jillian left his side abruptly. No other words passed between them.

On a bright Monday morning in Advent, Jeff arrived at the office early. With the press of the season now upon him there was much to do. During the next 44 days he had several special services to perform as well as a community concert in which to officiate. A December wedding was also on the schedule. He was somewhat anxious about his pending 10 AM appointment, but he was a bit intrigued as well. He was glad that Jillian would be at her position teaching this morning and not in the church. While she had not displayed any signs of possessiveness since they started casual dating, he wasn't sure what to expect from her. He wasn't even sure what to expect of himself in this situation either. Ernaline had him fascinated. There was much about her that he wanted to know. He also was curious about her intentions and her reasons for seeking an audience and any short-term, or possibly, long-term counseling with him. Jeffrey had lived long enough and had sufficient experience to become quite adept at listening, and as a direct counselor, offering advice. He did not particularly like being a counselor, but he was more than capable. He was actually, very proficient at it. One member of the congregation had said to him, "The difference between you and many ministers is that you really care!" This was true – he knew himself to be a very empathetic individual. He just hoped that in being so, he would not allow himself to slide into a troubling situation.

Ernaline arrived promptly on time. Jeff's secretary, Verna, who was a very friendly and a delightful receptionist, showed her to his office.

Verna knocked at his door and said, "Father Jeff, your 10 AM is here!" Turning to Ernaline, Verna said, "May I get you any tea or coffee, dear?"

"Thank you, but no thank you, I am fine," replied Ernaline politely.

"Thank you, Verna," replied Father Jeff, "that will be all!"

"I'll just shut your door and get back to my duties then," stated Verna staring at Jeff and making eye contact with him as if to let him know that she was nearby, if needed.

"Good morning, Father Jeff, how are you doing this fine day?"

"I am well and very pleased to see you today. How are you doing and how may I help you?" queried Jeff without hesitation and trying to get straight to the point.

"I am also fine, and very much looking forward to talking with you," Ernaline responded.

"Please, have a seat here in front of my desk. Make yourself comfortable. May I take your coat?" asked Jeff.

"Yes, please," replied Ernaline.

Ernaline took off her coat slowly as Jeff approached to help her with its removal, after all he was very much a gentleman. Drawing close to her from behind, he was able to get wind of her scent which was exceedingly pleasant to him. Realizing that this could be a compromising encounter, Jeff decided to sit behind his desk putting a barrier between them rather than sitting in a more casual arrangement as he usually did with those who came to talk with him at his office.

Their time together passed quickly. Jeff could not readily identify any particular issues she was having in life. She seemed more interested in his life and personal status than anything else. She also plied him with many questions about the church and where she might fit in. Her interest seemed real. She also indicated to him that she would be attending the special Advent evening services and musical events celebrating Saint Barbara and Saint Nicholas. When their hour was up, she sought to make an appointment with him for the same day, at the same time, the following week. As they stood to part, she approached him and wrapped her arms around him giving him a big hug. Pressing her body against his, Jeff realized that this was not just a friendly gesture. It was also not one in which she was expressing relief or out of a cry for help. Her clasp of his body was one that most people would think was too close, one which bore an inordinate amount of physical contact. It was, in a normal understanding, way too inappropriate. Her embrace of him was a significant one. In other words, it seemed to communicate much meaning. It was also one in which he noticed that something strange seemed to pass from her into him. A feeling, maybe, but it appeared to be something more than that – something spiritual, yet tangible. He just couldn't put his finger on it or describe it. He was alarmed by both her passionate embrace and by the sensation of something which came from her and seemed to enter into him. At the same time, he took some satisfaction in her embrace as well. He returned her coat and helped her put it on. As he did, she swung around so that they were immediately face to face. Jeff then took a step backward and made a gesture toward the door. He opened it for her and bid her a "good day." He watched her move down the hall toward the entrance. She turned her head somewhat seductively back toward him with her hair flying delightfully about as she presented to him a parting smile. Jeff thought to himself, "My, this woman is a big flirt." In all honesty he enjoyed their time together reviewing the encounter in his mind over and over again as the day went on. A conflict began to arise in him as he tried not to entertain any fantasies about her, but most assuredly he was looking forward to being in her presence again.

While Ernaline began showing herself at the church's special evening Advent services, it was not until the next Lord's Day that things became really interesting – and not so much with Ernaline, but with the reaction Jeff's friends, Chappie and George, had to her.

Ernaline continued on this particular Sunday to make a rather inviting and enticing presentation of herself. The whole congregation could not help but notice her, so much so that Chappie and George thought they might share with Jeff a few words about their observations after the service. Their mood and manner were couched in the humorous, but it belied a growing concern about the woman and her intentions with their friend. Stepping back into the unoccupied sanctuary following Ernaline's rather flirtatious farewell to Jeff at the door, George said to Jeff and Chappie, "My, that woman is something else! Where does she come from? What do you know about her, Jeff?"

Without giving him time to answer, Chappie declared, "A woman can be cute, attractive, appealing, pretty, and all together lovely; and then there is beautiful, drop dead gorgeous, exquisite, sultry, sensational looking, totally sexy, alluring, striking, seductive, voluptuous, foxy, fetching, and a whole bunch of other words in my vocabulary with which I could use to describe her."

"You are correct, Chappie," interjected George, "that woman is very fine-looking, eye-catching, and winsome. I imagine she turns a lot of heads."

"More than that, George," countered Chappie, while making sure that Lucy was not in ear-shot of the sound of his voice, "she is enticing, captivating, beguiling, and most beddable."

"Fellows – fellows, let's not go down that road! Let's keep this conversation appropriate and befitting our ethical standards," declared Jeff. "What is it you want to say to me?"

George spoke up. "Jeff, there appears to be something remarkably enchanting and fascinating about this woman. The words I would use about her are dazzling, fanciful, and bewitching. Chappie is right when he uses the words 'captivating' and 'beguiling'. She appears to me to be an enchantress. I think there is almost something hypnotic, mesmerizing, and magnetic about her. Yes, indeed, very much so. You need to watch yourself. She could certainly lead you down a path you will regret. And what about Jillian – your relationship with her – and her feelings? Have you taken her person, thoughts, and reactions into account? You've got a wonderful girl there with her; neither of us want to see you blow it! Danielle is also indicating to me some concern. Beware this woman. There is something about her that is just not right. I can't put my finger on it as yet, but she gives me the 'willies'."

"Yeah," said Jeff. "Thank you for your interest, gentleman. I will take your concerns under serious consideration. Now, if you would please excuse me, I must get on with this rather busy day of mine."

Jeff knew that they were right. He must exercise caution, but he was already at the stage of weighing his relationship with Jillian with that of a possible one with Ernaline. Of course, this was now becoming a point of stress and anxiety in his life – something he knew he did not need, but something he was not sure how to handle or from which he could escape.

Monday morning once more rolled around, and Jeff was looking forward with great anticipation to Ernaline's visit.

He found himself mulling over the possibilities that he might encounter with her and what might play out in real life. When she arrived right on time to his office, Jeff greeted her heartily with joy written all over his face. It was that obvious, obvious enough for Verna to pick up on his delight causing the good secretary just a little bit more concern as to where things were going with these two. The visit was a positive one with both of them laughing and joking and finding great humor in their conversation. Nothing of any import was discussed, though Ernaline did entreat him once more about membership in the church. Jeff found her to be delightful and she was, as usual, dressed in a stunning and striking manner. He had a hard time keeping his eyes off of her, though he tried not to be too obvious. It wasn't until the hour had evaporated that the visit took a spirited turn.

As Ernaline arose to depart she took a deliberate step toward Jeff, who was no longer sitting behind his desk, and said, "I want to thank you for seeing me. The time we spend together is so valuable and important to me. You are a marvelous individual and you are helping me, believe me, a great deal. I like to think that we are becoming great friends, and I really appreciate you." At this point Ernaline continued her approach to him, but instead of enveloping him with an embrace, she placed her hands on him and kissed him on his lips once, and then twice. When Jeff showed no hesitancy, she continued to engage him in a kiss that was both deep and passionate.

"There," she said to him with a sparkle in her eye. "I've got to be going now, but assuredly I will see you later – I am very much looking forward to continuing this with you. Good-day, now! Think of me!"

With that she was out the door. Jeff on his part was not sure what to think. The thoughts that were immediately running through his mind he found rather disturbing. Her kiss had certainly lit the fires of passion within him. There was also something remarkably different about the kiss he just received, and the one he entertained on the piano bench with Jillian a number of weeks ago. He was unsure how to describe it to himself. Ernaline's kiss was a burning one. It was a kiss full of unbridled and passionate lust. He even felt as if his lips, with the joining of hers, had slightly seared his skin. It was so discomforting, that it almost hurt. There was also no expression of love in it. With Jillian, the kiss, while an expression of the amorous, also communicated a great deal of tenderness. If he were to employ the wealth of Koine Greek vocabulary here for the one English word 'love', Jillian's kiss was that of agape and phileo - not just eros. It was a caressing union which spoke greatly of an unconditional personal regard, respect for the other person's character, and a caring affinity in the best quality of biblical love. There was a certain degree of sweetness to it – not one of painful desire. Jillian's kiss also possessed electricity. Jeff found it difficult to describe, but it was an intense feeling of conductivity – a wrapping – a binding together that was very appealing with a sense of righteousness to it. Ernaline's kiss was pure fire. Jeff was now very much concerned. His emotions were testifying to him that he desired to have Enraline and to surrender to her advances. His more rational self, put forth the question, "Is this what I really want?" The inner conflict was becoming a war – and with war there come casualties.

A Date, The Park, and Other Things

Jeffrey James did not stop seeing or conversing with Jillian during this period of time. Obviously, the two of them had to work together, but they also shared some personal time with each other outside of their church responsibilities.

One such occasion was a dinner date to a dimly lit and quiet restaurant. Sparsely crowded and much to themselves, Jillian decided that this was a good opportunity to confront

Jeff about her feelings and perceptions. Speaking softly but resolutely, she said to him, "You know Jeff, I have a great deal of admiration and respect for you. I really like you, and I'll be honest with you – maybe I shouldn't say this to you right now – maybe I am acting foolishly, but I deeply care for you. More than that, I have grown to love you. There it is – completely out in the open – I LOVE YOU," Jillian stated with emphasis. "I hope you love me too. And, if not, I hope you can speak these words to me one day very soon even if you cannot express this sentiment to me now. But Jeff, I really do not know where your heart lies. I thought I knew, but at this moment in time I am not so sure. I am not sure of anything between the two of us right now. You have taught me, through your Sunday messages and the teachings you give at youth group and Bible study, that love is both a choice and an action. You have taught me that choice and action come first in a loving Christian relationship – and then the emotions and feelings follow. You have shared with me the good words of Dr. Anthony Campolo that a man and a woman in love need to do the things that lovers are supposed to do. I guess that love is an act one makes a decision to creatively perform. I have very strong feelings for you Jeff, but my feelings come out of a heart of love for you. These feelings derive from a choice that I have made, and from actions that I have already shared to love you unconditionally if you will accept me and my love for you. I am here for you now and always, as long as you decide to choose me – just me, Jeff! Do you understand what I am saying to you?"

Jillian, wiping a tear from her eye, was beginning to choke up. She drew silent with her head bowed and her hand outstretched with her index finger pointed upward indicating a pause in her speech. Jeffrey, being a bit aghast, was

uncomfortable with the direction this conversation was going, but he knew he had to say something. "Wow, I didn't
realize that you are this far along in our relationship," he
replied hesitantly and with an air of caution.

"Just how far along are you with me?" Jillian charged
with some emphasis to her question. Without giving Jeff time
to answer, she continued, "I think we were advancing nice-
ly in our relationship until a few days ago when that other
woman appeared in church. Since then, I have felt a real distance between the two of us. There is a gap that appears to
be growing, not from me to you, but from you to me. Let me
ask you directly, are you interested in her? Would you rather
be in a relationship with her than me? Are you already in
love with her? Would you rather that I make it easy for you
and just break it off with you? Well, I am not going to do that.
I am going to make it tough on you. Yes, she might be sexy,
seductive, and sensual, but you'll never find another woman
who will love you as much as I do, and can, and will!" Slowing
down the cadence of her speech and speaking more tenderly
now, Jillian continued, "Jeff, you are a remarkable person.
You are a talented minister. You are adored by the adults
and especially by the youth. You are kind, caring, warm, and
have a heart of gold. There is, however, something about her
that is cold, calculating, self-centered and, perhaps, even cru-
el. She is just not right for you. I can see it, Jeff. I can sense
it! I can feel it! You need someone who is genuine and real. I
am genuine and real! I don't know what she is, who she is, or
where she came from – but there is something about her that
is fake and false to me. This includes any pronouncements
or actions of affection she might have made toward you and
whispered into your ear. Again, she's no good for you. I know
you. We've shared a lot together in the few months we have

known each other. Forgive me for saying this – and I am not trying to be pushy, but I believe that any woman in a relationship today has just as much right to be as forward and outspoken as a man. I think that you and I are meant to be with each other. I don't know if this is God ordained or not. How are we supposed to know that anyway? What I do know is that we have more than a love connection. We share deep spiritual convictions as well. You are more than my soul mate – you are my forever. I want to walk with you in the beautiful meadows of the New Heaven and New Earth and drink the sweet wine bursting forth from His Majesty's vineyards in the New Jerusalem. I don't know what there might be of marriage in heaven. I don't think the Bible is as clear on this subject as some people seem to believe. What I do know is that I think I will love you even more there than I do here, and certainly more than this very minute." Shocked and surprised at her own boldness, Jillian fights back the tears and says, "Boy, am I really making a fool of myself."

"You're not making a fool of yourself," Jeff immediately responded. "I just don't know what to say in response to all this. Our relationship is a young one – a new one – I haven't been thinking as deeply about this as you obviously have. I am sorry!"

"Just let me ask you one thing, Jeff, and I want the truth," Jillian stated with more determination in her voice than Jeff had ever heard from her before. "Are you conflicted? Are you conflicted between the two of us – her and me? Well, answer me, are you?"

"Yes, Jillian, I guess that maybe I am - perhaps," responded Jeffrey in a softer tone of voice.

"You guess – you guess – you don't know?" questioned Jillian assertively.

"I'm sorry, Jillian, I don't know what to say to you right now!" he stated in a frightened, but downcast and defeated manner.

"I should break if off with you right here and now, Jeff," asserted Jillian, "but I am not going to do that. I want you to really think on this and to pray about it. I will want an answer from you very soon, however. You are not going to be dating the two of us at the same time. I will not permit that to happen. I will not allow you to do that to me. I will not tolerate it," she stated emphatically. With a sad tone to her voice she continued, "I think I am going to skip the rest of this dinner. I am not feeling well. Please, I want you to take me home. Before you do, I want to make one thing crystal clear about where I stand with you. Jeff, I want you to be with me and I want, very much, to be with you. So please, select me, choose me, pick me, love me, be with me," Jillian stated pleadingly. Lowering her voice and tone she then said, "Forgive me and excuse me, but I'd like to go back to my apartment now."

Departing from the restaurant, Jeff drove Jillian to her residence. Few words passed between them on the return trip. It was an awkward drive for both of them. When Jeff stopped in front of her apartment, he promptly parked the car and planned to get out in order to escort her to the door. As he began to do so, Jillian said to him, "Please stay put, I can find my own way to my own door. There is, however, one thing I would request of you right now, please take my hand and let me say a prayer for the two of us. Most of the time we start and end our dates in prayer, just as we do when we share a meeting together at church. You know, come to think of it, we have prayed a lot together. I think we need prayer now more than ever. We certainly need God's involvement in this sad situation."

Jillian offered her hand to Jeff, and Jeff took it. Then Jillian began, "Lord God, I need your help – we need your help. Father God, in your goodness and providence, please help us with this relationship. I don't know if this relationship comes from you or not. I do not know if we are meant to be together or not. Whether it is in your hands or in ours, I ask you to assist us in the circumstances in which we find ourselves. Please heaven, hear our prayer and come to our aid. Please grant us guidance and show us the way. Please come to us and personally deliver us from any evil. Please God, help us to resolve this situation. Heal us, God no matter what happens – no matter the outcome. Lord, we need your help. Please hear our prayer. In the name of Christ Jesus, I make my request. Amen."

Before Jeff could say a word or add anything to the prayer, Jillian took back her hand. Her beautiful blue eyes were moist and glittering as she smiled broadly at him in what was much more than a mere glance. She then said to him sweetly, "Thank you for praying with me. I do love you so". With that she teared up, and made haste out of the car and to her door.

Jeff was very moved by her prayer, but also by the way she looked and smiled at him in that brief moment before she left his vehicle. Tears welled up in his eyes, making driving difficult. She was wonderful, unique, and extraordinary, and he knew it. How could he possibly reject her and let her go? Only a fool would do so. At that moment he thought of himself as one big foolhardy idiot. "Oh Lord, dear God, please help me," he prayed. "Don't damn me for hurting your dear one so. Please visit me and settle this thing. Please show me the way. I truly need your help, direction, and guidance. I am torn between the two. I need you to reason with me to help me decide. Please, Lord God, do not be far from me in this time of need. Please, dear God, come and speak to me. Please, just this once, God!" he said emphatically, almost shouting. "And God, please comfort my dear Jillian. Her heart is breaking. I alone am the cause of all her agony and distress. Forgive me, God! Please God, be attentive to her in this hour, through this night, and in the days to come. Sweet Jesus, attend to the needs of your servants. Amen!"

That night, Jillian had a difficult time sleeping. She was simply beside herself during one awful restless night of tossing and turning, weeping and wrestling with her inward anger and emotions. Since it was Saturday morning, she decided to get in touch with her best friend Danielle. She just had to talk things over with someone who might be able to provide her with some comfort, clarity, and direction. The two of them met together at Harrison Hills Allegheny County Regional Park in the chilly December morning, walking and talking, but mostly sitting on top of a picnic table. Here Jillian updated Danielle on the whole sordid affair in which she found herself.

Danielle listened intently to Jillian who went into great depth about the situation and what she was going through personally and emotionally. After Jillian had exhausted herself with the details of her heart and mind, Danielle responded without attempting to employ old cliches and oft-used phrases to placate Jillian.

Danielle began, "You know, Jillian, I do not know the biblical Greek language, but I can read commentaries, the Koine Greek dictionary, and Greek language lexicons and interlinears. I participated not long ago in a seminar with some of my friends on the subject of marriage. I even audited one course at the seminary in Highland Park last summer which detailed each and every Bible reference on this subject. The course covered the creation accounts, the Song of Songs, Ephesians chapter 5, and many other passages. You know Jillian how interested I am in all things biblical and theological. Even though I am very young, I have come to know a great deal about this subject and I think I need to share some of it with you now. Did you know that the Greek language used in the New Testament has four different words for our one English word translated "love"? Biblical Greek is a rich language and is able to classify into categories what we must take precision and care to interpret. If someone says to you, 'I love you', we have to interpret their meaning. In some cases that might be good, fine, and wholesome. In some cases, it may not be so. In New Testament Greek the different shades of meaning are quite clear. One word in the Greek language, as I understand it, was not often employed in ancient times. I think it meant a variety of things to a variety of people. The earliest Christians seem to have adopted and employed it as their one word representing the kind of love that God exhibited in Jesus Christ and, in particular, his action on the cross. That word is 'agape'. No one knows how the ancient Greeks actually pronounced this word, so my pronunciation of it may be in error. While there are some scholars who take exception to what I am about to share with you, the best translation and understanding of the word just may be our word, 'sacrifice'. The play on the Greek words for love becomes important in Peter's and Jesus' conversation in John 21:15-23. One cannot totally understand the meaning of the passage without knowing the Greek words that are uttered back and forth by the two of them. They spoke, of course, in Aramaic, but the story is related to us in Koine Greek. Knowing which Greek word is being used is important all over the Gospels and Epistles. One of my favorite passages in the Bible when attempting to understand the relationship between husbands and wives in Greek Christian culture, comes from Ephesians chapters 5 and 6. Now, I know that you and Jeffrey are not married, and what applies here is only to women and men in the sanctity of marriage, but I think it still has great application to your situation. Personally, I am looking at this passage with great interest myself."

"How so Danielle?" asked Jillian.

"Well, you know that George and I are seeing a lot of each other," said Danielle. "He asks me to get together with him to study French, and then when we set a place and a time, he comes up with suggestions to go and take in a movie, a play, a concert, or some other event or activity. And so off we go in Margery. Margery, by the way, is the name of his car. He names his vehicles, mind you. He is one interesting dude, is he not? He also writes me beautiful letters and notes, he e-mails and texts me frequently, and he enjoys talking with me on the cell phone. What he shares with me is often very humorous. He is one interesting guy who is full of all kinds of noteworthy observations and ideas. He is never, ever dull! I think he is in love with me and I bet he asks me to marry him very, very soon. I can feel it coming."

"If he does, what are you going to say to him, Danielle?" asked Jillian. "Are you in love with him too?"

"I don't know, Jillian," responded Danielle. "I certainly like him a lot. I have never met a finer man. I love spending time with him. He is, assuredly, growing on me. I think – well, I think if he asks me, I would have a difficult time turning him down. I'm not sure if I am ready to marry just yet, but at the same time, I might respond in the affirmative trying to convince him that I might need a long engagement. Seriously, he is just too good to lose. I know he is not the kind of a man women dream about, but I have never met a person who has been so good and kind and true to me. I like him more than any other person I have ever met. He is always right there when I need him. He supplies anything I might need and he has this uncanny ability to know what I need before I do. His anticipation is amazing! But enough of this, we are here to discuss your situation, not mine! You know, Jeffrey is a great guy too."

"Oh, you are so right, Danielle," replied Jillian. "That's what makes this situation so difficult for me. Like your Tuey, he is the finest man I have ever come to know. I think I would just die if I have to give him up. At least, something inside me would die, I think."

"Do you know what, Jillian, your relationship with Jeff is still fresh and new. You've only been together for what? – about two months or less, right now," surmised Danielle. "You've got to give this guy a break. This whole thing might actually work in your favor. It is forcing him to deal with his feelings and his relationship with you. He may come out of it with a great determination to hold onto you and to love you. If he doesn't, then what good would have it been anyway? You may not be as physically stunning as that other woman, but you are quite a catch, my friend. He would be a fool not to choose you, just like I probably would be foolish if I turned down a man as remarkable and personable as my Tuey."

Danielle then returned to her main line of reasoning, "Ephesians chapter 5 and proceeding into chapter 6 deals with Christian house rules in terms of three specific relationships in the ancient world, which are somewhat different, but still applicable today. The first of these, concerns the relationship, in Christ, between a husband and a wife. Please understand that this is not talking about the relationship between men and women – it is strictly about how wives and husbands are to conduct themselves before Christ in the marital union." Danielle, with conviction and intensity continued, "The topic sentence of this passage has been greatly ignored. It declares that before Christ, our relationships with each other are to be conducted under mutual submission. The wife is called by Paul to 'submit to her husband'. At that time in Greek Christian society such was often not the case, and Paul is adding the corrective here. Some of this situation might deal with temple prostitution; paganism on steroids, but that's a conversation for another day. What Paul is communicating to his readers, in other words, is that God's will for the wife in a Christian marriage is to put the needs, wants, and desires of her husband before herself. Her task is to concentrate on him and to serve him. Paul then adds, 'in everything'. We are to understand that 'everything' means 'in all things that are godly' and in accord with the dictates of biblical values, ethics, and morality. If it – a behavior, action, or even an expression - is not godly, then that changes this injunction. God and God's precepts and dictates always come first. Just when some husbands get giddy with this text, Paul continues. He charges the husbands to 'love their wives'. Now, at this point most women cry foul and say that there is a big difference between the words, 'submission' and 'love'. Is there? Not according to the Greek. The Greek word used here is – you guessed it – 'agape' – which in Christian circles usually means 'sacrifice'. What Paul is calling the husbands to do is to 'sacrifice" themselves for their wives. It is precisely what many husbands in Ephesian society were not doing and he calls them out on it. The husbands are not putting the needs, wants, and desires of their wives first and foremost in their lives. I know it sounds like a typical man, but Christian men are not to be the typical men we often experience in this world."

At this point, Danielle put her arm around Jillian as they continued sitting on the picnic table. "George and I have discussed this passage. He agrees with what I have learned about it," stated Danielle. "I am so happy that he is very open to biblical study on so many things, including matters of relationship."

"Please continue, I am so happy that you have learned all this material and that you are so willing to share it with me. I find this very interesting, especially due to my circumstances," stated Jillian.

Happy to be affirmed, and that Jillian was interested in the subject, Danielle continued, "Paul then proceeds to the topic of 'headship'. Now, I have studied this. 'Headship' in Greek has two main streams of understanding. One set of meaning deals with the Western concept of – well, let's say, military rank – captaincy – headquarters - from which all orders are cut and flow. This is where the debate comes into Christian family circles about who is in charge – the husband or the wife. This has led to much confusion and an outright rejection of this text. It is here that society and culture has made a great assault on the Christian Church. It is here that biblical advocates have failed miserably to defend it. To many, it has become an embarrassment. The reality of the matter is that there is a second set of interpretation which understands headship as the 'source of blessing.' Only by understanding the context does the reader know which interpretation is in play. Now, I could go into more depth on this, but suffice it to say that the context indicates that the husband is supposed to be the 'source of blessing' for his wife. He is to shower her with love, goodness, blessing, and provision. This passage has nothing to do with 'who is the boss and who is in charge.' Christian marriage is much more challenging than that. Both the husband and wife are called by God to serve the other. The wife is to sacrifice herself for her husband. The husband is to sacrifice himself for his wife. Their relationship is one of giving and not demanding and taking. It is truly all about servanthood – mutual servanthood. No one is in charge in a Christian marriage save for Christ. Christian marriage is much about sharing and caring and dialogue and sacrificing and coming to a mutual understanding that both can live with happily. The blessing pronounced on such a binary relationship of mutual giving is that the 'two become one'. In other words, they grow so intimately close to each other that their relationship becomes a spiritually rewarding and deep composite unity. This outcome reflects the unity evident in the divine Trinity. There is so much more going on with God's gift of love than humanity really knows and can comprehend. This is where I think your situation comes into focus."

"What do you mean?" asked Jillian.

"Granted, you and Jeffrey are not husband and wife – but you need to be a good steward over this relationship and exercise Christian servanthood," asserted Danielle. "Before the two of you were lovers, you were a sister and a brother in Christ. He needs you to serve him by being present for him, talking with him, sharing with him, not giving up on him, helping him to see the truth – whatever God might declare that to be. He needs you to pray for and with him. He needs you for care and understanding during this difficult period he is going through. Sure, the sin of lust, and whatever else, might be getting in the way and plaguing him. You need to stand ready to forgive and grant him the gift of grace just as he needs it from the Christ. You need to put away some of your own emotions and feelings of injury about this, and help him through this troubling season for both of you. The benefit for you – and for him too – might be that he sees your godliness and embraces the love you have to give him. Right now, he needs an under-shepherd to the greatest Shepherd of all. 'Paraclete' with him. In other words, 'come alongside him to help'. Be his strength and guide. If he is the person, and I mean righteous person, that I think he is – he will turn once again to you, embrace you, and love you forever. I really think he will. I'd like to say that I know so – but both of us understand that God has to do a work on his mind and his heart. Frankly, Jillian, I do not think our God will be wanting. I firmly believe that our God is God. He cares for both you and Jeffrey. I have prayed earnestly that God gets directly involved in this situation and guides it to a good out-come. Why don't we pray right now for divine intervention and a godly ending!"

Jillian and Danielle lock both of their hands in prayer. Instead of bowing her head, Danielle raises her eyes to the sky and utters a praise and faith filled prayer for assistance to God. Her confidence in God strikes Jillian as most remark-able and it ministers to her downcast soul. In fact, God's Spir-it, through Danielle, has ministered to Jillian so effectively that Jillian leaves the park with renewed strength and an uplifted countenance.

At this juncture in our story all that is missing and neces-sary is God's response. What is God going to do? How is God going to respond? What course will God's interaction take? A number of people are waiting on God to find out just that!

Stave 6

Re-entry

It was a beautiful time in the "Intermediate Heaven", but then all time is marvelous in God's "Paradise" for the saints prior to the Second Coming, The Bodily Resurrection, and the gift of the Eschaton. Heaven is a busy place. It is a place of great energy and bustling activity. It is a place and condition that does not know the meaning of the word, "boredom." The archaic ideas of floating on the clouds, winged saints, and harp playing is as alien to heaven as fire extinguishers are to hell. All the time, God's business is being conducted by the Trinity, by the angelic host, and by the saints. There is much work to perform and everyone is eager to accomplish it. Some of the cosmic activity is in response to circumstances and issues on planet Earth.

At one particular moment in divine time, three very poignant prayer requests were marked for immediate attention and sent down the chain of command. Quintas, the angel in charge of handling some of the more interesting prayer requests coming up to heaven from Southwestern Pennsylvania, received a communique noted as being one of "Special Priority." Receiving the telepathic communication from those with greater access and a higher clearance to the Cosmic Office, Quintas composed his own telepathic message to one of his angelic subordinates. The message communicated stated, "Rasmus Gilbert Feynman is to be beamed into my office immediately - without delay. Regardless of any other tasks he is engaged in currently, he must present himself to me at once."

Communication in the intermediate heaven is almost instantaneous. Within what would count as seconds on earth, the former Father Feynman was present and accounted for before Quintas.

"My good saint, it is a pleasure for me to finally meet you," stated Quintas with a cheery voice.

"It is good to finally meet you too, as you are an angel of great distinction and responsibility," replied Rasmus politely.

"You are probably wondering why you have been summoned by me," remarked Quintas as he began to pace back and forth. "I have a heavenly assignment for you to fulfill. This one comes from the very top. We are sending you back to earth once more in a ghostly form. Once again, you will have the ability to materialize and be given all the necessary tools to accomplish your mission."

"Where on earth am I going?" asked Rasmus.

"We are sending you back to Southwestern Pennsylvania – to the northeastern most corner of Allegheny County. You know the area well. You are being assigned to the towns of the Highlands and Freeport districts: specifically, to Freeport, Natrona Heights, Brackenridge, and Tarentum. You accomplished your last assignment with great skill and a terrific sense of purpose. You did not violate the boundaries that we set for you, and so we are giving you once more this opportunity to serve His Majesty in this new endeavor. I hate to inform you of this, but you are going up against your former nemesis again. She is on the loose attempting to create havoc through a new strategy – that is a new strategy for her, and I only use that pronoun loosely – for she is an 'it' from the infernal bowels of the Luciferian rebellion. I believe that you referred to her previously as 'The Lady of the Church'."

"That is correct," replied Rasmus.

"One of the things that failed to happen in your former assignment was to take care of her permanently. This time we want you to lock her up until Judgment," Quintas declared.

"My, my – going up against that confounded troubling demonic entity again, am I," said Feynman rather matter-of-factly.

"Intelligence confirms that we must respond in a more direct way on this one." Quintas continued, "The difficulty takes place in another Anglican Christian Church which is actually a new church development above Freeport. You would not have any previous knowledge of the establishment of this church due to the time difference between heaven and earth. This church has a long title; "The Church of the Incarnation and the Saints of Advent." The rector is much like you when you were in Saxonburg, and also much like Father Freeman. He is a very righteous man and we want him to stay that way. His person, and the character of the church he serves is sincerely endorsed by the Cosmic Office. They do not want this congregation to become yet another failure spiritually, theologically, morally, and practically. There is a great need for this kind of Church in the communities that surround it, and so direct involvement has been ordered. You, my fine saint, are the action figure we are sending out to help influence this situation toward a godly end. The rectors' name is Father Jeffrey James Fairlamb. In your previous life the two of you never crossed paths. Hey, great name, isn't it? We in heaven here like it to be sure!"

"Yeah," interjected Feynman, "anyone with a name like that needs to be saved!"

"Precisely," stated Quintas, "but, of course, that is not why we are engaging this operation. Your 'Lady of the Church' has made herself incarnate and goes by the name Ernaline Bedelia Kherington."

"Wow, that's a loaded name," exclaimed Rasmus.

"It certainly is," agreed Quintas.

"We are loading her file right now into your mind so that you have access to everything – which is literally, everything, we have on her - it" expressed Quintas with a chuckle.

"She is using her artificial feminine assets in order to have Jeffrey succumb to temptation to take him down and the church with him. You must try to convince him of her origin and status. He must overcome and throw off this temptation.

There are also some other human agents involved in this troubling situation. Two of them are female. The primary one is known as Jillian Julianna Jiganie. She is the church organist and is involved with Jeffrey – not overtly sexual as yet, praise be to Providence for that, but she is deeply in love with him and most concerned. She is a sweet and tender lady, but willing to put up a good fight. I think we can count on her to help convince Jeff of the trouble he is in. Her prayer for direct help is the first one we registered. The other female agent is her best friend, Danielle Dayanna Gadberry. Her prayer is the third registered one that came our way. She knows the Word and has given her friend quality counselling and advice."

"You missed one registered prayer there, Quintas," exclaimed Feynman.

"That one came from Fairlamb himself," stated Quintas. "He is much conflicted, but loves the Lord. I think you can show him the truth, help him to correctly identify the enemy, and engage in spiritual warfare. Combat of the spiritual kind is going to be needed by both of you." The specialist on the Southwestern Pennsylvania prayer response emergency team continued, "You will be making two visits. Your first one will be to Jillian Julianna Jiganie. Like before, you will be briefed telepathically and given all the spiritual tools needed to fulfill your assignment. Then you are to visit with Fairlamb. Currently it is the cultural Christmas season on earth. We hope you can clear up this mess prior to their recognition of December 25th. Are you ready to find yourself on Earth again?"

"Yes, I am, if need be," declared Feynman resolutely.

"Good," exclaimed Quintas. Going on, Quintas added a reminder, "Ah, one more thing, like before you may not reveal yourself to anyone you knew previously and that includes your family."

"I know," stated Feynman with firmness in his voice. "I am ok with that now – knowing heaven and the future, well, it has a way of making one glad even during a period of separation."

"Now be off with you, my good saint," charged Quintas.

"Yes sir," snapped Rasmus giving Quintas an earthly military type salute.

Your God is God

Rasmus Gilbert Feynman was returned to his ghostly form and transported across the dimensions back to planet Earth. His assignment was to visit both Jeffrey James Fairlamb and Jillian Julianna Jiganie. Between the two, he was ordered to appear to Jillian first. From what he knew of the situation, he had a greater emotional attachment with Jillian. He thought it wise to comfort her before heaven had him tackle what he thought might be more of an intransigent stand from Father Jeff.

It was night. The strength and confidence Jillian felt in her conversation with Danielle had faded somewhat. She found herself in constant agitation over this whole situation. For her there seemed to be no peace. Certainly, there was no escape. The only solace she discovered was in prayer. The words to the old hymn, *What A Friend We Have In Jesus,* certainly rang true in her heart at this time. She discovered that singing many of the old hymns of the Church seemed to reinforce and uplift her failing spirit. She was raised on a greater diet of the contemporary Christian music scene, but when it came to a time of personal strife, the older, more traditional hymns seemed to speak more directly to her heart and to the circumstances in which she found herself. The lyrics of each old hymn became a sermon testifying to her to trust in Christ.

In the darkness of her bedroom, she knelt down beside her bed like a child getting ready to say his or her night-time prayers. In quiet desperation she began her petition once more to heaven. "Dear God, I am here again trying to confidently wait upon You and Your time. Forgive me, but I am having such a difficult task in so doing. I am just sick and heartbroken over this whole situation, and I am unhappy with myself. Why did I give my heart so readily? Why did I give my heart to this man who might cast it aside and reject all that I desire to give him? I really need to know what you want me to do right now, even if I might not want to face the final consequences in store for me. I have petitioned you so many times over the last several days and yet all I seem to get is silence. It is as if my prayers are bouncing off the ceiling of this bedroom. Maybe you aren't listening, God. Maybe you aren't even really there."

Just at that moment, Jillian was stunned and startled to hear a response. "Jillian, your God is God," a voice declared emphatically as it reverberated through her tiny bedroom. For her part, Jillian collapsed to the floor both in fright and in amazement. She wanted to stand and turn on her overhead ceiling light, but she felt paralyzed. She thought it best not to try to move. Listening, the mysterious voice continued, "Your God, sweet child, has heard your many prayers. Your God has seen your tears. Your God feels your brokenness. Your God is now responding to the many pleas that have been lifted up by you, and for you by others."

The bedroom light was no longer needed. A dazzling display right before her eyes began as a pin-prick of radiance, and then rapidly magnified itself until it revealed a luminous figure. The form glowed brightly, then dimmed as it took on a physical manifestation. It still bore enough light that Jillian could easily make out its features. Remembering the stories in the Bible of divine visitation to women, Jillian determined not to jump to conclusions predicated on fear. Just then the mysterious figure pronounced the words repeated oft in the Word, "Fear not Jillian, for I have been sent to you from God to help procure the outcome of the matter which concerns you. I am here to bring this situation to a divinely desired resolution," stated Feynman who had yet to introduce himself.

"Sir," stated Jillian forthrightly, "might I inquire as to your name, station, and the precise nature of your business with me." Jillian was always known to be rather bold and outspoken in her speech. While she was truly a sweet young woman, she was not afraid to speak her mind. She could be very direct, and she could really deliver a severe scolding to someone when she deemed it appropriate. Even though she was diminutive in stature, she was a real firebrand. Having put aside her initial fear, she was ready to conduct business with this messenger from heaven.

"My name is Rasmus," stated Feynman

"That's an interesting name for an angel," mused Jillian.

"Well, let me correct you, I am not an angel," stated Feynman directly and clearly.

"Then what are you?" replied Jillian. "Speak up and inform me of your heavenly position!"

"I am a spirit – the ghost of a human being dearly departed," stated Rasmus

"Wait a minute," interrupted Jillian. "I did not think that once deceased – and whatever people talk about 'passing over' – that human spirits could return to earth."

"You are mostly correct on that assumption. I, and other human spirits like me, on certain occasions when strictly engaged in the conduct of divine business, are permitted to return in ghostly form, or in a more tangible form as I have now taken before you," explained Rasmus. "This is only my second such assignment. Such a circumstance is indeed rare. Please allow me to fully introduce myself to you. My name on earth, and I still retain the same identity today, is Rasmus Gilbert Feynman. When I died accidentally – well sort of – I was the fairly young rector for Holy Trinity Anglican Church in Saxonburg. I left behind a wife whose name is Laurel, two children: John and Janet, and my beloved dog, Kinghorn."

"What do you mean by 'sort of' in terms of your death?" inquired Jillian. "Did you come to some foul end?"

"Yes, I did," asserted Rasmus. "I experienced a dread confrontation with a demonic entity who was indirectly responsible for my fall through the tower room of the church and down onto the chancel below."

"A demonic entity aided in your demise?" reiterated Jillian with surprise and some trepidation.

"Yes, and I hate to inform you of this," stated Rasmus with hesitation, "but that same foul phantom is very much involved in the situation in which you are now suffering."

"But I haven't encountered anything demonic, save for this certain disgusting woman who has come into my life and is really messing it up," stated Jillian.

"Bingo," responded Rasmus with a shout! "The one you know as Ernaline Bedelia Kherington is the materialization of a very significant demonic entity whom I have termed as 'The Lady of the Church.' She is a most diabolical fiend – even more of an unclean familiar spirit than most in that realm. She means to do Jeffrey and his church much harm. In fact, she means to destroy both him and anyone who gets in her way. My dear child, you have gotten in her way. She will attempt to destroy you as well. I do share some concern for you, my sister. Since *The Church of the Incarnation and the Saints of Advent*, is a significant threat to the dark forces in this area, her assignment is to neutralize it and make negligible its influence. I have appeared to you for three reasons. The first reason is to provide you comfort in knowing that His Majesty is certainly aware of the situation and has engaged heavenly forces to respond. Heaven also wants you to know that while the one you love is under great temptation, he is also being demonically oppressed both inside and out."

"What do you mean by that – what you said, 'both inside and out'?" questioned Jillian.

"There is more than one demonic entity involved in this crisis we are facing." said Rasmus with determination. "A number of entities have been forced inside of him. I would not say that he is 'possessed' because he is a man full of the Spirit of God, but they are there to attempt to influence his decisions. Why do you think that the demonic entity came to him in such a sultry and seductive way?" asked Feynman rhetorically. "When she first embraced him, she passed into him her evil minions. My dear, you've got to understand, that these things rarely operate alone. The term, 'Legion' as a reference to them is spot on! Jeffrey is responsible for his decisions, his sin thus far, and any other sin he entertains in this situation, but you must understand that there are mitigating circumstances in this predicament. Your friend Danielle is correct, you must grant him some sympathy and mercy. He is going to need your grace and forgiveness. He may also need your help."

"What do you mean? How can I help?" asked Jillian, not sure if she wanted to hear the answer.

"You are one tough woman, Jillian. Heaven knows that," stated Rasmus. "We know of your determination and that you have a stubborn streak. Your stubbornness may serve us well in this situation if you can muster the courage to engage in combat in a spiritual way. Evil is crafty, potent, and capable of messing up the people and things of God. What God's people need to understand is that evil does not possess the authority that God's children already have and can exercise at their fingertips. You, like me my dear, are God's steward created and called to perform mighty works. In the name of Providence – in the blessed name of Jesus – you have great capability. I am going to give you a tip here in case you ever need to employ it. All demons hate hearing the name of 'Jesus'. The pronouncement of the name of Jesus absolutely terrifies them and can make them take to flight. Anything, even common things, blessed for use in the name of Jesus and by Jesus and his stewards, can be employed as a powerful weapon. Remember that, my fair one!"

"Wow, you've given me a lot to digest here, Rasmus," stated Jillian as a smile broke out on her face. "What now?"

"I think I have said all that I need to say to you at this moment," stated Rasmus. "You may, or you may not, see me again. Be well assured that I will make a good attempt to be near you if at all possible until this situation is resolved. I will try my best to assist you if trouble comes your way. Right now, I must leave you and appear before Jeffrey. Please pray for me to our heavenly Father, for what I must now share with him is going to be more difficult than what I have had to explain to you. You have received my words with greater faith, understanding, and acceptance than what I may experience with him. My time with you has been most encouraging and pleasant. I thank you for that, my child!"

"Wait a minute, what happens now?" asked Jillian.

"I don't have full knowledge of that, except I know that we have got a battle to engage and win! Stay in an attitude of prayer and may the Spirit be with you and guide you through these coming hours. I've got to deal with Rector Fairlamb now. And then Rector Fairlamb has got to do much of the lion's work in assisting me with – well, you know who," finished Feynman.

"God speed, Rasmus, and please do me one thing," Jillian said with tears welling up in her eyes.

"What is that my dear child?" queried Rasmus.

"WIN," pronounced Jillian emphatically, shouting the word.

With Jillian's assertion, Rasmus instantly disappeared. The room was once more totally dark, but it was not without light. A new, bright luminary, was shining throughout Jillian's being and spirit. She was now on fire for God. She paused for a moment to think over her encounter with Rasmus. A big smile suddenly captured her face as she then declared to herself, "Yes indeed, my God is God!"

Stave 8
She's a Man Eater

Upon leaving Jillian, Rasmus immediately began his ghostly flight to locate and confront Jeffrey James Fairlamb. With identity recognition and location information provided to him spiritually, he knew he would find the good rector working late in his office at the church. Rasmus pondered how to make his presence known to the hard-working, but conflicted priest. He decided that some sort of grand presentation should accompany his arrival.

Rasmus flew through the walls of this new construction and entered the sanctuary. His first reaction, which he said to himself as he looked around was, "Nice Church." Then taking on a physical form and emanating some light while still suspended in the air, he called out to the young pastor. "Jeffrey – Jeffrey," he spoke forth in a loud voice.

Jeff, for his part, was sitting at his desk doing some paper work. He was surprised to hear a voice coming from the direction of the sanctuary, or so he believed. Wondering who was in the church at this hour, he rose from his desk to investigate.

Rasmus continued calling Jeff. "Jeffrey – Jeffrey," he said again, "Would you please come here?"

Entering the nave, he was startled to see a luminous figure adrift in the air in the very center of the room. "Who in the devil's name are you, and what do you want with me?" he asked the hovering phantasm in a frightened voice.

The phantom responded by saying, "You should be asking me, 'Who in God's name are you?' I have been dispatched by heaven with an abundance of information I am required to share with you," stated Rasmus in a booming voice which echoed off the walls of the sanctuary.

"How am I to know what you are telling me is true?" questioned Jeffrey. "For all I know you could be a figment of my imagination, the result of a chemical imbalance in my body, or something coming from the dark side."

"I believe I can convince you of my person and my mission in due time. Allow me to introduce myself properly to you", responded Rasmus.

Gliding toward him now, Rasmus landed between two pews in front of where Jeffrey was standing. Jeff took a couple steps backward, but determined not to flee as the phantom approached. Taking on full physical form and dowsing his glowing radiance, Rasmus spoke to him in a softer, more congenial manner. "Have you ever watched the 1940's Jimmy Stewart movie, *It's A Wonderful Life*? Well, I'm your Clarence, except I am not an angel and this circumstance is without a hint of humor."

"No, I haven't seen the movie. I don't watch the ones that are only in black and white," stated Jeffrey in quite a frank way.

"Too bad, it's a good one! Like the character Clarence in this movie, I have been sent in response to prayer - more specifically, your prayer, and that of both Jillian Jiganie and Danielle Gadberry. Please allow me to introduce myself. I am Father Rasmus Feynman, formerly of Holy Trinity Church in Saxonburg, now resident of the intermediate heaven."

"Are you the spirit of the priest who fell to his death a few years ago? I heard about that. Good Lord that was most tragic," said Jeffrey with an air of sympathy.

"Yes, I am the ghostly materialization of that priest who has been sent on this mission of divine visitation," replied Rasmus slowly. "I have been permitted to take my previous form so that I might assist you."

"Assist me with what?" queried the good rector.

"Don't you know, my fine man?" responded Feynman. "You sir, are in a very bad way. I do not think you know how dire your situation is and the extent of the trouble in which you currently find yourself." stated Rasmus firmly. "So here I am. I am the answer to your prayer, my good fellow. You prayed and you got me! In other words, God has enlisted me and sent me to aid you – more specifically – to rescue you."

"I don't need rescuing!" stated Jeff defiantly. Curious, he then asked Feynman, "Rescued from what?"

"Your real question needs to be, 'Rescued from whom!'" countered Rasmus. "You need to be rescued from a demonic entity that is attempting to destroy you, your work, your relationships, and this church. And, my good fellow, you need to be rescued from yourself."

"What are you talking about, and what demonic entity are you referring to? There is no demonic entity here or in my life," asserted Jeff. "And I am doing just fine myself, thank you!"

Rasmus responded, "It is an 'oldie' as some refer to it. It is from the 1970's. Have you ever heard the song entitled, 'Devil Woman'?"

"No, I haven't and what's that got to do with your visit to me?" asked Jeff.

"Well, the lyrics to this song in your situation are instructive. It goes something like this: 'She's just a devil woman with evil on her mind. Beware the devil woman, she's gonna get you from behind,'" stated Rasmus melodiously. "You've got a sure-fire devil woman on your tail good man, and you're not paying any attention to what is really happening."

"Come on, don't jest with me," exclaimed Jeffrey.

Rasmus continued, "The song goes on and says, 'Be careful…of a lady with long black hair, tryin' to win you with her feminine ways.' Is there anyone in your life that matches that description?"

"Well, no, there isn't," stated Jeff with some hesitation as if he was hiding something.

"Are you sure? Certainly, there is," replied Feynman answering his own question. "Her name is Ernaline Bedelia Kherington. What do you know about her? Where did she come from? Where does she live? Did she ever provide you with an address, e-mail, or phone number? Did you ever try to follow her? Does she even drive a car? Have you ever seen her anywhere else, but here in this church? When she leaves here, assuming she does, where does she go? What does she do? Do you know anything, really, about her at all? Her name, Jeff! What about her name? Do you know what her name means? If you don't, you should, it is very informative! 'Ernaline' means 'capable', 'serious', 'and one who will battle to the death.' 'Bedelia' means 'powerful', 'strong', an 'exalted one.' 'Kherington' means 'she has sprung from the fire.' Do you know anyone with stranger names than that? They communicate a message, Jeff. She, through her name, is signaling who she is and what she is. She is telling you her very nature. Can't you see it, Jeff? Don't you feel it, Jeff, when she is with you? Don't you sense fire in your soul and a burning sensation in your body when she is around you, embraces you, and kisses you? Hasn't she set your passions on fire? Isn't your lust burning red hot when she is in your presence and when you think of her? Pay attention, man – you have got to start resisting her advances and your own carnal urges, re-orient yourself with God, fight back, and eliminate her from your life. Jeff, she is not real. She is not human. She can never give you what you truly want, need, and desire. She can't – she is not even a woman – she's an 'it' – a lousy demonic evil force. You think she is absolutely gorgeous. What she shows you is just a shell, a façade, a stage prop. If you only knew what she really looks like, and you just might find out, you would be not only repelled, but sickened through and through. Once more, what you want is reserved for another, and you know of whom I speak. In addition, how are things going here ministerially? Haven't you been greatly distracted lately? The whole congregation knows it. They see what is happening, and some of them believe you are thinking with – well, let's just say – they think you are not using your brain."

"Oh my God," shouted Jeffrey in an awakening to the realization of his plight. "Rasmus, my problem is that I do want her so. I feel her not only with me all the time, but also inside me."

"That's not by accident, my good man," asserted Rasmus. "She has intentionally implanted something evil within you, which we must get rid of, and fast," declared Rasmus.

"I really don't know if I can let her go, but I do realize that you might be right," Jeffrey said agreeing hesitantly.

"Trust me, Father Jeff. Trust heaven. Trust also in God. You must take authority over those trying to destroy you; command them now and put to flight any unclean spirits within you. You must. And you must do it right now," advised Feynman.

"This is hard for me. It's hard for me to let her go," replied Jeffrey.

"Jeffrey, let me ask you this question, whom do you really love? For whom do you have a heart of tenderness, a genuine liking, a sense of deep camaraderie, a depth of spiritual connection and feeling, a sense of comfort and belonging, who is absolutely a joy and so much fun to be with? Admit it, like you admitted it to yourself when you slid off that piano bench some weeks ago."

"How do you know that?" Jeffrey replied with surprise.

"Hey Jeff, heaven knows everything. Nothing can be hidden from God.," instantly responded Rasmus. "You love Jillian. She is your soul-mate. She is the one who is right for you. You two have come to a meeting of the heart and mind, and God endorses the choice you have made in her. Search your heart and soul, you know she is the right one for you. You know, when in your right mind, that you have already made this decision and chosen her. Is this not part of the genesis of the entire turmoil you now find yourself in? Am I correct? Am I not telling you the truth?" asked Rasmus. "You know the truth. And you know what you must do about it! This woman – this it - is a man eater, a relationship destroyer, and a church undertaker. I have named her the 'Lady of the Church'. My title for her, however, is far too dignified for her true essence and character. There isn't anyone or anything that it, and the evil it represents, won't kill and bury. What do you say? You know the prayer of personal cleansing and deliverance. Don't you think it is time to use it? There is no better time than right now. I am sharing heaven's thoughts with you on this subject, Jeffrey. Your first love has always got to be Jesus Christ. Jesus is calling you back right now. Jesus wants you to fully embrace him again. It's time, and believe me, there is no time to lose."

At that both Rasmus and Father Fairlamb entered into prayer. Rasmus was pleased that Father Jeff was easier to convince than he had otherwise feared. Father Jeff confessed any sin he might have committed, particularly that of lust. He confessed the hurt that he caused to God, Jillian, and those in the church. He asked the good Lord to bestow grace upon him and restore him to a right relationship with the divine. Praying in the Spirit, he took authority over any untoward entities oppressing him and commanded their departure and removal from his person. He also commanded their departure from the vicinity of those whom he loves and shepherds, including the church and the community. He requested the Holy Ghost to give him a fresh in-filling of the Spirit, and to permeate God's church here on Freeport Hill.

As he was praying, the two saints of God heard grunts and groans; moaning and sighing. Father Jeff, also felt something depart from his body as his torso convulsed with some involuntary movements. As the prayer ended, Fairlamb looked up at Feynman.

Feynman then said hurriedly, "Prepare yourself, Jeff! With her minions no longer attached to you she is aware of a disturbance in her evil force. She is coming to you right now. You have got to stand up to her and defeat her. Remember, with God all things are possible. You can cast her aside and away from you and yours forever. Do it! Also, do not let her trick you. She is going to try! Remember to whom you belong and to the ones you really love! I am now going to meet her, then you must entertain her, employing God's might and authority. Put on the armor and stand ready for combat. God will be with you and will not forsake you."

"I am afraid – very afraid," stated Jeffrey nervously.

"You know," responded Rasmus from the historical library of his memory, "your attitude needs to be the same as a certain American commander in the Battle of the Bulge when the Germans had him surrounded and sought his surrender. Do you what he said to the Germans?"

"No, I don't," replied Fairlamb.

"He gave them only a one-word reply. He wrote down the word, 'Nuts' on a piece of paper. He was telling them to 'go to hell.' That is what you must say to the one coming to visit you, and you must send her there," stated Feynman emphatically.

"Where are you going to be when I tell her where to go?" asked Jeff nervously.

"Don't worry about me, I know what I am doing. Just make sure you stand resolute," charged Rasmus.

Stave 9
Nuts

Rasmus ended his conversation with Jeffrey and took to flight out of the sanctuary and into the entranceway of the church. He positioned himself behind the two doors leading from the outside into the narthex.

Jeff, at the same time, nervously retreated to his office. He was not sure where he should meet Ernaline if, in fact, she did drop in on him.

It did not take long for the double doors to suddenly burst open even though they were locked. Ernaline, dressed in a most seductive manner, entered the church with what appeared to be a violent wind circulating about her. The breeze she caused resulted in a number of items taking to flight about the narthex. There among the motion and the commotion, stood Feynman with a big smile and not a concerned look on his face at all.

When the Lady of the Church recognized him, she too smiled, but her facial expression was more like an evil grin. "I'm back," she said to Rasmus.

"And so am I, you murderess," stated Feynman with complete derision in his voice and on his face.

"I guess it is fitting that the two of us should meet once again on the field of contest," chuckled the vixen without any sense of fear. "I'm here to deal with that idiot and foolish rector of this nauseating place," Ernaline said vindictively. "He's another one of these clueless followers of, well, you know who."

"You just can't say his name, can you?" Feynman said with a laugh.

"Now, don't give me any of your lip, I've got a meeting with his minister-ship. Between you and me, we'll see what he decides, and whom he chooses. I can be quite persuasive. I always bet on me. Just stay out of my way!" cried Ernaline with confidence.

"Go right ahead, foul spirit," stated Feynman, "I'm not even going to try to stop you or hold you back, and neither am I going to curse you in your attempted endeavor." Confident in the fortitude and veracity of the young rector, Feynman continued, "Go ahead, take your best shot and let's see what happens."

With that Feynman vanished. Ernaline checked her appearance in a near-by mirror and proceeded toward Jeff's office. With each step she took, she attempted more and more to take on the character she desired to portray to Jeffrey. By the time she got to his door, she was fully immersed in her acting.

Knocking on the office door, she called out, "Jeffrey, are you in there?" She did not wait for an answer, but immediately she pointed her finger and the door swung open. She then stepped into the threshold, and leaned against the jamb in a very sexy and sultry fashion. "Good evening, my dear," she purred. "I bet you are surprised to see me, but I just couldn't stay away from your manly presence even at this late hour. I'm here for you, Jeff. You can have me, Jeff. You can have me all to yourself. I know that you want me. Here alone at this time in this building, its perfect for us to get better acquainted, don't you think?"

"That's the thing, Ernaline. I am now really thinking," he stated with emphasis, "and I do not believe that you should be here with me right now. It's just not right!"

"Of course, it is right," retorted Ernaline. "What is wrong with you and I getting to know each other a little better. After all, I think we are meant for each other."

"Meant for each other," repeated Jeffrey with raised voice. "What exactly do I get for being with you and embracing you? I am not even sure that you are human. Are you human, Ernaline? Can you prove to me that you are, and not someone or something from perdition?"

"I'll show you how human I am, and in the process, you'll get all of me and these," she replied, as she began to expose to Jeffrey her upper torso.

"Stop, Ernaline," he commanded. "Are you even real? Is what you are trying to show me even real?"

"Of course, I'm real, and well, there is no better reality for you than what I can give you, right here and now."

"I don't think you are human at all," Jeff charged with some trepidation. "You are something completely alien – your precise identity is the only remaining question I have, though I think I know of your origin," as Jeff tried to get her to admit her true essence and derivation.

"Of course, I am human," she stated. "Who gave you the idea that I am not human, that creepy little busybody ghost who gets into everyone's business? Don't listen to him, he's the evil one here. What makes you so sure that he is not trying to mess up a goodly, godly, divine thing between you and me right in this moment? Can you be so sure that he is not your real foe? Look at me, do you think this is evil?" She ran her hands up and down her curvaceous body. "Baby, I'm good – why don't you come over here and find out for yourself? I'll show you the truth, and a real good time as well!"

"The truth is that I know who and what you are," stated Jeff with conviction. "You are a demonic entity known to some as 'the Lady of the Church'. You are a destroyer of persons, relationships, and ministries. Your aim is not to love me, but to compromise me, neutralize me, and maybe to even destroy me. It is time we part ways. You may take your leave, or I will be forced to…."

With that, not another word came out of Jeff's mouth. The foul creature had a supernatural grip on his larynx so that he could not speak at all. "Forced to do what?" she asked him. Jeff then found himself levitating about three feet off the floor. In another instant he was slammed against the wall behind his desk. There he was pressed fast against the vertical surface while still suspended in the air. Ernaline started to walk slowly and seductively toward him and swung her body sensuously around his desk. She stood right in front of him just a couple inches away. Looking up at him, she placed her hands on the belt that went around his waist. Jeffrey was thoroughly afraid of her next move, but he was powerless to do anything about it. All he could do was to give her what disgusting and revolting facial expressions he could muster under her tight grip. He did not want her to force herself on him. Fortunately, he could tell that his message of total derision for her was now beginning to register.

"Oh, so you don't want me now, do you?" she spat with disgust. "I was good enough for you to lust after, but now when it comes time to really play ball, you're not interested. Oh, I see, you want the scrawny little 2 by 4 who sits her petite ass on the piano bench with you. Have it your way, but I am going to make sure that you are not going to get her. Do you realize what you're going to lose with me? Do you realize what you are giving up? Together, we could really be something, Jeffrey. Together, we can accomplish remarkable things. I want to infiltrate you with my love – to possess you with my ardor – to hold onto you tightly – to complete you – to reside with you and in you - to be one with you. I can show you a whole new world. I can show you a whole new life, far more spectacular than the one you are existing in now. Why don't you give up and just let me?"

Struggling to talk, Jeffrey who was still suspended in the air, wanted Ernaline to loosen her grip around his neck to let him speak. He motioned to her to do so. Knowing the danger in the words that he might pronounce, she released her grip only just enough to allow him to be heard, ever ready to pinch him off again. "What are you trying to do, make a devil out of me? You can't possess one filled with the Holy Spirit. I serve another who has blessed me abundantly and eternally. It is God whom I choose to serve, and Jillian whom I determine to love."

With that Ernaline's hair began to move forward from her head toward Jeffrey's face, touching it, and caressing it – up, and down, and around. He could smell her wondrous scent that had previously intoxicated him. Suddenly the strands of her hair began to thicken as if she were Medusa with her head of snakes. The scent of her hair turned foul as well. At this moment, Jeffrey had never been more frightened in his life.

"Is that all you have to say to me?" bellowed the entity as her snake-like hair projection returned to her head.

"No, there is one more thing, 'Nuts' to you, you witch bitch – go to hell!" Jeffrey cried.

With that, Ernaline tightened her demonic grip on his throat and cut off his ability to speak. "Have it your way," she shouted. Right before Jeffrey's eyes he witnessed her transformation into something absolutely grotesque and hideous; an accurate reflection of her true essence. Gone was the woman who portrayed herself as an earth angel. Feynman was right, truly she was a devil. Revealed right before him was a despicable and thoroughly monstrous figure. The being was entirely ugly and thoroughly gross both inside and out. Dropped was any pretense of being the seductive Ernaline. She was replaced by the true hideous portrait of the Lady of the Church. No longer in bodily form, the demonic specter in a complete tantrum cast a spell detaching and throwing around all sorts of items throughout the church building. Cut loose from its moorings, items big and small went crashing about, making the once beautiful church nearly a complete mess. As she did so, her spirit flew close to Jeff with mouth growing larger and larger as if she would swallow him whole. Stopping just in front of his face, she looked him square in the eyes and said, "I am going to take you down and your little pretty too, in fact I am going to mess her up and make her uglier and more grotesque to you than I am right now." Screaming and shrieking as in a whirlwind, off she went exiting from the church and sped off into the dark night.

Jeff had no opportunity to pronounce the words of deliverance he had hurriedly prepared as he understood Feynman's prompting. She had been wise to shut him up. She did not release her grip upon his esophagus until she had departed church property. Once he fell to the floor, all he could do was to get up, attempt to catch his breath, run out of the church, jump in his car, and drive like he was at a motor speedway to Jillian's apartment. He figured that he would find her there. All the time he pleaded with heaven repeatedly to allow Feynman to run interference. He also prayed that he could get to Jillian in time to save her from harm, evil, and injury.

Stave 10
This Ain't a Hallmark Movie

While Jeffrey James was speeding down the highway to get to Jillian, his nemesis had already arrived on the scene. Jillian was in bed as it was late in the night, but could not sleep. Her anxiety about Rasmus' visit with Jeffrey, Jeffrey's response, and an attack by Ernaline on any of the three of them kept her on edge. Following Feynman's

appearance to her, she had spent some time in prayer petitioning God to assist Rasmus and Jeffrey. She prayed might-
ily that Jeffrey would be able to throw off the temptation
which apparently plagued him. She hoped for the best, but
feared the worst. She also possessed a great deal of anxiety
about coming under demonic assault herself. In her prayer
she pleaded with God to give her the spiritual weaponry she
might need to defeat the enemy if such an attack came upon
her. As she continued petitioning God, an inner voice that
was not her own said to her, "Fear not my child, for I am with
you. This battle is mine. Trust in me and you will see My
salvation." Jillian was a bit rattled as to the origin of this lo-
cution, but strange happenings were now nothing new to her
on this particular night. Trusting that the voice was divine,
she begged God to give her both the needed wisdom and
knowledge at the right moment to know what to do and what
to say. Nervously, she huddled in bed pulling up the covers
around her head. Sleep, however, abandoned her as she was
captive to her thoughts and to her anxieties which even the
divine message could not relieve.

Retaining invisibility, the foul fiend entered Jillian's bedroom. Suddenly, the entity pulled back the covers from Jillian's bed and conjured up a blast of frigid air and cast it upon
her. With the blankets ripped out of her fingers, Jillian became very fearful. Wearing a warm and colorful pajama out-
fit, she wondered how her blankets had been wrenched away
when she could not see or hear a thing. She reached for her
bedstand light switch and turned it on. Looking around her
room, there was nothing she saw that was out of the ordinary.
Unsure what to make of this, she slid out of her bed in order
to pick up her sheet and blankets. Precisely at the moment
she bent down to pick up her bed covers, she heard cackling

and laughter. It grew louder and louder as she dashed toward her bedroom door. Immediately, an irresistible force hit her and threw her back on her mattress, pinning her down with enormous authority. Greatly astonished but defying her fear, Jillian spoke to the invisible monster by employing the name of Jesus and by commanding it to get out of her room. Her counterattack worked. Released, she immediately thought that the best thing she could do was to vacate her apartment. Quickly grabbing the keys to her car, she fled from the scene.

Jillian sped away traveling north in the direction of the church and Jeff's residence. As she did so, the fiend took on a hideous form and flew after her car. Through her rearview mirror Jillian was startled to see something wild and scary flying behind her in the darkness. It was closing in upon her fast. In an instant it was beside her on the driver's side door, keeping pace with her advancing speed. Making monstrous facial expressions at her through the window, the beast also produced terrifying shrieks and high-pitched sounds. Jillian knew that she was in trouble. She also knew that she had to keep her cool. She couldn't panic. She had to keep thinking clearly. Quickly, she came to the conclusion that the beast would probably try to force her into some sort of an accident. Wrecking her car and possibly gravely injuring herself or another person became another frightening prospect. This instantly dominated her perplexed mind as she tried to escape this monster.

Just then another speeding vehicle passed her going in the opposite direction. Surprisingly, this caught the attention of the entity. The unclean spirit broke off chasing her, abruptly stopped, and began spinning around and around right there in the middle of the highway. Jillian wondered if it were trying to determine which car to follow. Jillian also wondered if the other speeding vehicle might be Jeffrey. She thought she recognized the car, and the driver appeared to be a solitary male figure. A number of options instantly presented themselves to her. She pondered whether or not she should head to one of the local police stations. There were three of them separated by only four or five miles. She could also attempt to find an open store and intermingle among the people there. Realizing, however, that she was in her pajamas without a coat, she decided to reverse course and try to catch up with the other speeding vehicle in case it might be Jeffrey. Trying to find Jeffrey in order to face this ordeal together was something she dearly hoped to secure. Having made her decision, and with the entity presently nowhere in sight, she pressed down hard on the accelerator.

In so doing, she passed by a local police cruiser which had just pulled off by the side of the road. The patrol car's lights and siren immediately came on and began the pursuit. Looking for a place to pull over, Jillian wondered if the officer's attention would be helpful or detrimental. As she was slowing down in order to stop, an airborne figure looking like a Halloween witch, flew toward her windshield and up and over her car. Behind her, in an instant, she saw the police cruiser go high into the air and then tumble to earth with a great thud, turning upside down. Terror-stricken, Jillian tramped hard on the gas pedal. Rocketing out of there, she passed by the intersection nearest the entrance to the hospital. She instantly grew disgusted with herself and slammed her hand on the steering wheel. The hospital was a place she could have taken refuge. "After all many people arrive at the hospital at night wearing all sorts of things," she thought to herself. Instead of going back to the hospital, Jillian reasoned that if that had been Jeffrey who passed her a couple of minutes ago

- "He's probably going to my apartment." Making a quick 90-degree left-hand turn at the next street while almost upsetting her car, she sped toward her residence. Jillian pulled up and stopped suddenly. In the parking lot she spied Jeffrey's automobile. Jillian did not see him in his car. "Where, in God's name, is he?" she exclaimed. Suddenly, there was a great thud as two hands appeared on her passenger side window. Jeffrey pressed his nose up against the pane and shouted to a startled Jillian, "Let me in." Jillian unlocked the car door and Jeffrey quickly jumped in.

"Let's get out of here," he said to her. "It isn't safe here and you are in great danger."

"What about you?" she shouted at him.

"Never mind me," he retorted. "What are you doing up and driving around this late at night? I was really worried when you did not answer your door and your car was missing."

She said to him as they sped away, "It has already been to my apartment and I was able to escape. I was driving in an attempt to find you!"

Jeffrey exclaimed excitedly, "It has already been at the church, and I too have escaped when it decided to leave me and come after you."

"What does it want with me?" Jillian shouted.

"It blames your love for me for wrecking her plans, and so it wants to repay you with evil. She really wants to get you," stated Jeffrey in a loud voice. "She means to mess you up, disfigure you, and maybe even kill you."

"Can it do that, Jeff?" Jillian responded. "I mean, God wouldn't allow that to happen to me, would He?"

"I don't think so," Jeff stated, "but it contributed to Feynman's demise so we can't take any chances with this thing.

Regardless, we've got to find refuge. In all likelihood we are going to have to confront it again. If we do, we have got to be bold. We have got to act quickly. We must also permanently expel it from our presence. Look - driving around like this is way too dangerous! I'm afraid we're going to kill ourselves or someone else," Jeff exclaimed.

Having driven rapidly down the hill into the flats of Brackenridge, Jillian made a right turn and was heading toward Tarentum. As they traveled down First Avenue, Tarentum Riverview Park along the Allegheny River came up beside them.

"Here," shouted Jeffrey to her. "Let's stop at the park and see if it shows up."

"I don't think we can hide from it," offered Jillian. "You should have seen what it did to that police car coming after me!"

"Police car! What are you talking about? You had a police car chasing you?" asked Jeffrey excitedly.

"Yes, and the foul thing threw it up into the air and crashed it," exclaimed Jillian. "I hope the officer is not injured or dead," she offered. "Why didn't it do that to stop us?"

"I don't know," said Jeffrey, "but I hope we are flying under some divine protection. Frankly, I'd like a lot more divine protection and also some big-time heavenly intervention right now." Gazing upward, Jeff shouted, "Come on God!" Turning to Jillian he exclaimed, "Where in God's good name is Feynman's ghost? Where is he when you really need him?"

Just at that moment a fierce and very foul wind blew through the park.

"It's here!" said the rector in a low voice, ducking down in his seat. Immediately, he reached over, grabbed Jillian, and pulled her down as well.

The moment Jeff finished lowering Jillian completely down onto the front seat, the car was picked up and hurled in the air down the street. It came to a crashing and sudden stop amid a great amount of noise on the old yellow brick boat ramp that led down into the Allegheny River.

Smelling gasoline, Jeff shouted at Jillian to get out of the car while at the same time hoping that neither of them had been greatly injured in the crash. Unfortunately, there was no time to make a personal injury inventory. They ran down the boat ramp toward the river and then tightly embraced. As the two of them looked up the ramp, the vehicle suddenly exploded into a ball of flames. Jillian placed her face into Jeff's chest, as she couldn't stand to watch her burning automobile. Immediately behind them they heard movement in the river. They turned to see a figure hovering above the water with the fire of the burning vehicle illuminating its foul image. Dressed in what appeared to be filthy rags, the dark green entity with stringy black hair flying wildly in the wind, peered at them with bright red eyes. It then expressed a grunt like a bull ready to charge.

Breaking his embrace with Jillian, Jeffrey spoke saying, "I've had enough of this!" As he begun to pronounce the words of spiritual warfare, he was immediately seized and thrown back quite a distance against the high stone sidewalls of the ramp entrance. Jeff's head hit hard on the rocky wall. The impact made it difficult for him to retain consciousness.

Jillian, though alarmed, was not frozen in fear. She was furious, and she bravely determined to do something about the evil this being was perpetrating against them. It had hurt her beloved. She was not sure of the extent of his injuries as Jeff slowly slid down the wall and settled to the ground. Suddenly the prospect of injury and death was inconsequential to her. Mustering all the righteous indignation she could, Jillian stared angrily at the entity hovering in the air near the shoreline as if she were now possessed by a greater force ready to discharge its power. Remembering Feynman's words, Jillian began to speak. The foul demon reached out its bony hand with its index finger pointed at Jillian to silence her as well. Only this time its powers failed. Heavenly forces were now intervening and had blocked its injurious magic. Jillian, sensing that a divine anointing was upon her, courageously pointed her index finger at the Lady of the Church and said, "I now command you in the blessed name of Jesus Christ to trouble us no more. I now bless the waters below you in the name of Jesus Christ to jump, crash and thrash upon you, roll you up, and expel you from our presence, taking you down river never to return to plague us again." At this, the waters of the Allegheny rose up and seized the wicked being, washed over her, and in a tumbling motion whisked it downstream in a torrent of water as if a dam has been breached and broken.

Jillian, full of great emotion and resolve rushed to Jeffrey, knelt before him, and then sat down, placing his blood-stained head upon her lap.

"Jeff, how badly are you hurt?" she asked with great concern.

"I took quite a hit, but I can see and hear. I hope it is not as bad as it feels and as it might look to you! Good Lord, I've taken quite a beating tonight. However, it could have been much worse," he said as he looked at her. "But Jillian, I had enough awareness to hear what you said and to see what you did. I've never seen anything like that before in my whole life. You are truly amazing. What a dynamo you are, my dear," Jeff stated in complete awe and with grateful admiration.

Without responding to Jeffrey's words of praise, Jillian said rapidly, "I've got to find a way to get you to the hospital, my love."

At that very moment, flashlights bathed them in light as two Tarentum police officers on night duty were now on the scene. Highland Hose and Eureka Hose Fire Companies could also be heard in a distance coming their way as well with much fanfare and noise.

"Are the two of you ok?" asked the police officer.

"Yes and no," stated Jillian. "I am not hurt, but I am not sure about my boyfriend here. He is bleeding some from his head, but he is fully conscious."

"EMT's are on their way and will be here shortly. I want to know right now what happened here and if you were driving under the influence. I need to talk to both of you and get some statements from you," commanded the policeman. "Is that your burning vehicle up there?"

"Yes, it is, officer," asserted Jeffrey "and we know that you need to talk with us. Rest assured that we are not under the influence of any toxic substances. We will certainly cooperate with you. Could you please give us a couple of minutes – we've just been through a lot, which we will try to explain to you in a moment. We just need some time to collect ourselves, and I have some things I must say right now to this young lady, after all the things we have just been through tonight."

"Alright," said the man in a dark navy-blue uniform, "but you don't have long. I've got to get to the bottom of this incident. Stay right where you are - where I can see you. Don't move! Don't leave! And don't try to get away!"

"You can trust us, officer - thank you," replied Jeff.

"How are we ever going to explain this to these officers and to the authorities?" Jillian asked Jeff. "They are never going to believe us. I think you and I are also going to be in trouble for the road violations we have made."

"Don't worry about that now, Jillian. I've got some things I must say to you right this minute," stated Jeff, as he looked up into Jillian's face with his head still resting on her lap. Continuing, he said, "The answers to your questions are, 'no,' 'yes', 'yes', 'and when the way is clear, yes.'"

"What questions?" inquired Jillian. "I don't have any questions for you!"

"Whether you realize it or not, you have four questions for me. The answers to your questions are: no, I will never allow myself to be tempted by another woman again; yes, from this day forward I will only have eyes for you; yes, I want to explore with you a long-term relationship; and yes, when the way is clear, I will marry you." Jeff expressed this to Jillian with an undeviating straight-forward resolve and all the tenderness he could muster.

Jeff then struggled to get up on his feet as Jillian helped to support his body. Standing erect, Jeff gazed into the lovely face of Jillian as the couple were illuminated by the light thrown off from the burning vehicle. Jillian began to tremble in her pajamas on that frigid December night. Quite cold, she was also reacting to the disturbing events she had just experienced. These happenings were absolutely terrifying, and the thought of what had just transpired made her shiver as well. Speaking to Jeff she said affectionately, "I love you, Jeff. If you are asking me to marry you, the answer is 'yes' – absolutely yes, yes, yes!"

"Yes, I am, Jillian. There is no finer person for me than you. I know that now. I would be a fool to ever reject you," stated Jeff with deep conviction.

Then Jillian said, "Hold me tight, Jeff. I am sorry I am shaking so. I wish you would say something funny to me right now. After all the things we have been through tonight, I could use some humor."

"Humor, you say – something funny, huh! Well, you know dear, this whole episode, in this particular season, reminds me of a Hallmark Channel Christmas movie," Jeff blurted out much to Jillian's surprise.

"A Hallmark Channel Christmas movie – how in the world do you come up with that?" she asked in a loud voice. Going on, Jillian said, "In this tale of ours there is no community Christmas tree lighting ceremony, there is no gingerbread house building contest, there is no Christmas caroling event, and there is no hot chocolate being passed out. These things all seem to be in every one of their seasonal movies. With all these things missing, how again is this like a Hallmark Channel Christmas movie? Would you please explain this to me?" inquired Jillian.

"Well, my love, how do all Hallmark Channel Christmas movies end? Don't they end with what I call the 'Hallmark Kiss'? You've heard me comment about that enough by now. Haven't you? Well here's my ending to this evening and our mutual beginning to a whole new life. Here's my happy Hallmark Channel kiss to you!"

With that Jeff approached Jillian's face with his own while placing both his hands on the sides of her head and the two of them locked lips. Sure enough, between the two of them, it was completely electric once more.

Stave 11

ᘙhe Consummation of the ᘙale in ᗽoth the ᗷresent and the ᖴuture

Cold air was being blown off the water, further chilling Jillian. As she and her beloved were embracing along the riverbank deep in conversation, a figure was standing to the side in the darkness just out of the light.

This figure was not a hostile one; it was in fact Rasmus – one of the friendliest ghosts in the heavenly realm. Rasmus was very pleased with the way his assignment had ended, except for one thing. Rasmus, however, unbeknownst to Jeffrey and Jillian, had been very involved in the events that played out. It was Rasmus who confused the fiend when Jeffrey and Jillian's vehicles had passed each other. Rasmus also eased the crash landing of Jillian's car on the former brick boat ramp just enough to keep the two from death and injury. It was Rasmus who cushioned Jeffrey's body just enough to keep his head from greater injury. The ghost on assignment from heaven also helped to block the demon's effort to silence Jillian. Finally, it was the late rector who added heaven's own supernatural power to the waters of the Allegheny to rise up and carry the entity in a fast current down river.

Rasmus decided that it would be a most appropriate act on his part to express team unity between the saints triumphant and the saints-militant if he stepped out of the shadows and strolled over to congratulate this couple and share in a parting expression. So, out from the shadows he approached the two in full bodily form.

"Hi," Rasmus said with a smile. "Congratulations I guess are in order. Happy engagement, you two! I must say that both of you were perfectly marvelous in the way you handled the confrontation tonight, especially you, Jillian."

"Wasn't she just wonderful?" added Jeffrey, who could not contain himself.

"She's a keeper, Father Fairlamb. You remember that and make sure of it your entire life," expressed Rasmus. "Treat her well and love her with everything you've got!"

"That is now my number one life priority other than Jesus, of course," returned Fairlamb.

"Of course," replied Feynman.

Rasmus then got down to business. "You two have got to talk to the police now. Jeff, they are going to send you to the hospital. Jillian, you will be going to the police station. The Tarentum detective will be talking to both of you together and separately. Tell the truth even though the authorities and the magistrate will not believe you. They will be unable to refute your story and so the whole incident will be dropped. You will, Jillian, have some trouble with your insurance company. Get a new one. See that fellow in the Heights who was a former auto salesman. I became acquainted with him through his brother who constantly teased me that I only worked one day a week when I lived in Saxonburg. He'll help you. I'll make sure of it," Rasmus expressed with confidence. "I have to go now. It was sure great to meet the two of you. I am happy I could help you. May God bless you always and in all ways!"

"Will we see you again, Rasmus?" asked Jillian.

"Probably not in this world," responded Rasmus. "But I assure you that we will meet again in heaven and be together in the coming new heaven and new earth. In fact, when you arrive, be sure to look for me because I'll be there to greet you. In the meantime, I will be rooting for you! Well, like that old song from many decades ago shared at a time of parting, "This is adios and not good-bye.""

With that Rasmus began to fade away. Both Jillian and Jeffrey shouted in unison, "Good-bye, Rasmus, and thank you! Thank you so very much!"

Rasmus was correct. The authorities did not believe Jeffrey's and Jillian's story. No one who heard it believed it, except for their closest friends. All traffic violations and any other misdemeanors were thrown out by the court. The Harrison

Township police officer whose cruiser was overturned miraculously escaped injury, of course, and the readers of this tale should know why. Jillian did have trouble with the insurance company, but her new agent became a saving grace in her life. The *Church of the Incarnation and the Saints of Advent* was a mess in the aftermath of Ernaline's tantrum. While Jeffrey told the Vestry the truth under a gag order not to reveal the contents of the report, some members of the Vestry were not so sure about his story and his interpretation of events. There was, however, no way they could refute it either. The congregation believed that the church had been vandalized, though ghostly stories about the circumstances abounded. All the remaining services that season acknowledging the saints, the remembrances, the Eve of the Eve service, and Christmas Eve and Christmas Day worship were held in spite of the damage to the church. Members of the church noticed, and remarked to each other, that there seemed to be a special sweetness in the atmosphere during this season. The church was blessed in that the same sweetness continued to linger as the seasons came and went.

Jillian and Jeffrey were married in the church sanctuary in early June. Eventually, they had three children – one girl and two boys. They gave their first son the middle name of "Rasmus", honoring the apparition that had been so influential in their early relationship. They gave their second son the middle name of "Gilbert", remembering how a saint from heaven had aided them in their time of great need. Jeffrey and Jillian served the church the remainder of their careers right up to retirement. It was one of the longest pastorates in Natrona Heights history.

Danielle married her Tuey. Yes, George proposed to her not long after Danielle expressed to Jillian that she thought he was going to pop the question. She hesitated and said to him, "I guess so." Finally, after several weeks went by, she did indicate to him that she, in fact, loved him. Danielle was a real blessing to Stuart George Duckstein. She kept him in line and fed him intellectually. He started to refer to her as "Boss Woman" and continued to call her that his entire life. Their marriage was a marvelous one as they enjoyed 47 years together. With as fantastic as their relationship became, it felt to them to be all too short as they reached their senior years. A life fully lived with worthwhile relationships, involvement in positive activities, and with meaningful pursuits will always appear to be short. Perhaps it would be wise for God's people to talk about this life as a "pre-life" to the life that is to come. Maybe our designation of life following this life as the "after-life" is a misnomer. The life that comes next may just be the real life that God intended for us in the first place.

Jeffrey and Jillian, along with George and Danielle, Chappie and Lucy, and Scheidy as well, became life-long friends who socialized together, frequently vacationed together, and shared a Bridge Club card playing night almost every week.

The Church of the Incarnation grew and thrived. It became known as the church in the region which celebrated the seasons – particularly Christmas, well.

Rasmus, upon leaving Jillian and Jeffrey at the river, decided to take a detour before returning to the transfer portal back to the intermediate heaven. He had been instructed not to make any contact with his family, but Quintas did not indicate that he couldn't drop in for a silent and secret visit. He found their home in Delmont and entered into the living room. There before the roaring fire in the hearth sat his wife Laurel reading while John and Janet were playing a game together. Rasmus' heart ached when he set his eyes on his beautiful wife – she was still young and as gorgeous as the day he married her. He marveled at how his children had grown in his absence. And there, laying by the fire was his brindle buddy, Kinghorn. Kinghorn had aged in his time away and was now an old dog. When he drew near to his American Staffordshire Terrier, the dog looked up. Rasmus suddenly realized that by some means the dog knew he was present. The dog raised up on all fours, tail wagging with an intensity the family had not seen in a long time, and he barked twice at what appeared to be a vacant corner. Of course, Rasmus was present there, though invisible to them. Feynman, with an invisible touch, gave Kinghorn a great hug and said to him, "It won't be long, my 'big dog', until we will be together again." Kinghorn's action and the peculiar movements around the dog's neck, sides, and back caught Laurel's attention. She smiled in the direction of Rasmus and whispered, "I love you", thinking that a divine visitation by her one true love might be taking place. Longingly, Rasmus stared at her for a while but could not tarry though he wished otherwise. Looking at Kinghorn who was intently sitting there sweeping his tail across the floor from one side to the other, Rasmus said, "You know, my boy, C. S. Lewis was right after all about dogs and heaven."

The next thing Rasmus knew, he was in the presence of Quintas once more.

"Nice job, Rasmus," stated Quintas, "except for one thing – one very big thing!"

"I know," interrupted Rasmus, "in our hurry to be rid of it, we failed to permanently take care it!"

"Yes," stated Quintas. "Do you know what that means?"

"I am afraid to ask," responded Rasmus.

"It means that you will be going back, my good saint, and this time…"

Rasmus cut off Quintas and finished the sentence, "I will be required to finish the job!"

"Correct, my good saint," said Quintas with a sharp look on his face. "I will be in touch."

"Of course, you will," replied Rasmus as he left the office.

About the Author

Robert Cameron Malcolm IV, is a 1973 graduate of Highlands High School, a 1977 graduate of Westminster College, New Wilmington, PA., and a 1981 graduate of Pittsburgh Theological Seminary. He served the First Presbyterian Church of Bentleyville, PA, for 6 ½ years. He then served the Natrona Heights Presbyterian Church as pastor and youth group leader for 30 years from 1987 until 2017. This book is his fourth. In 2018 he produced his first book, *A Unique History of Natrona Heights Presbyterian Church.* In 2020, he published his second book, *Mary Magdalene: New Testament Eve.* In 2021, he published his third book, *A Divine Christmas Ghost Story.* He is currently working on writing, producing, and publishing five more books. Cam, as he is known to most people, lives in Natrona Heights with his wife, Laurie Ann Wright Malcolm, and his son, Robert Cameron Malcolm V.

WA

www.ingramcontent.com/pod-product-compliance
Lightning Source LLC
Chambersburg PA
CBHW061635050726
47502CB00012B/2237